One Spark

"Imagination Begins with You…" 2022

One Spark
"Imagination Begins with You…" 2022

Compiled by Brianna and Levi Teel

This is a compilation of works submitted by high school students for the "Imagination Begins with You..." annual writing contest. Each story's copyright is owned by the author of that story and used by permission in this compilation. All profits from this compilation will fund scholarships for higher education.

Library of Congress Control Number: 2020940635

Cover design by Jasmine Mumford

Interior design by Jasmine Mumford and Brian Claspell

ISBN: 978-1-947315-10-5

ACKNOWLEDGMENTS

Many people have helped judge and make this high school writing contest possible. The stories have been phenomenal.

We extend our thanks to all of the judges: Natalie Daines, Malory Martin, Sarah Christesen, and Brian Claspell. A big thanks as well to all of the teachers and administrators who encourage their students to participate, and to all of the students who send in the stories. We extend a special thanks to Brian Claspell, who has sponsored this competition, and without whom this contest would not be possible.

2022 Winners and Finalists

Winner:
The Importance of a Speck of Dust
by Rebecca Lorenz

Second Place:
Michael the Archangel
by Samantha Hall

Honorable Mentions:

Lured   by Abbi Payne
Trove of Imagination   by Lydia Cooper
Words on a Screen   by Ara Colby

Finalists:

"A Colorful World" By Bailey Stender
"A Dream" By Jules Hau
"Desert of the Lost" By Adriane Navolis
"Diary of a Raincloud" By Chase Pickford
"Do You Have the Time, Sir?" By Adriana L. Robinson
"Evil, Senseless, Inhumane, Remorseless" By Maddox Umholtz
"Faith Can Stop a Bullet" By Bryson Bentley
"Fated (Not) to Last" By Erika Prophete
"GET COMFORTABLE WITH BEING UNCOMFORTABLE" By Lance Mathis
"Goodbyes" By Sofia Prieto Black
"Gone" By Callie Cooper
"Hiding from the Sun" By Alexandra Marie Chilson
"Imaginary Monster" By Sophia Ospina
"Journey to the Moon" By Isabella Dintino
"Jr. Year" By Emily Gard
"Just Corn" By Katelyn Carafelli
"Lured" By Abbi Payne
"Michael the Archangel" By Samantha Hall
"Miracles For Mateo" By Clara Wiggins
"Mysterious Puppeteers" By Evelynn Esparza
"No Matter What" By Lauryn Bickle
"Not All Heroes Wear Capes" By Natalie Rice
"One Forty-Nine" By Rowan
"One Last Time" By Kendahl Parsons

"R&R: Rice and Relationships" By Isabel Marie S. Auclair
"Rare" By Aurora Rutkowski
"Reaper" By Presley Roose
"Socks and Crocs" By Anna Mutzenberger
"Springs in the Wasteland" By Emily Peterson
"Sunday" By Rishi Makam
"The Artificer" By Mason Gabriel George
"The Chimes" By Kayla Maura Freedman
"The Creature Inside Me" By Nicholas D. Hagedorn
"The Doorbell" By Daniela Cantu
"The First Christmas" By Ashley Dawn
"The Girl With Moths in her Hair" By Chloe Thompson
"The Happiest Days of Our Lives" By Andrew Davies
"The Importance of a Speck of Dust" By Rebecca Lorenz
"The Last Goodbye" By Stella Walborn
"The Mournful Tragedy of Walter Dormio" By John Colby Andrews
"The Storm" By Rebecca Gardner
"The Toy Soldier" By Julia Bobe
"Trove of Imagination" By Lydia Cooper
"What Life is Really About" By Sophia
"Words on a Screen" By Ara Colby
"Work over Will?" By Morgan Smith

CONTENTS

SECTION 1 - MAGIC

A Colorful World

By Bailey Stender (Finalist)

There was once a little girl named Poppy that lived in a village in the valley of two mountains. The valley was full of lush green wild grass and towering pine trees. There was an abundance of wildflowers of every color from the brightest yellow to the deepest blue. Poppy loved to pick orange poppy flowers and bring them home because they had the same name as hers. The stream ran clear and pale blue and reflected bright pinks and purples at sunset and rise. Poppy loved to watch the sunrise the most and her favorite color in the sky was fluorescent orange.

Her family owned a bright red barn that Poppy loved to play in and see the animals. She had her own barn cat named Milo that was an orange tabby with wild green eyes. Milo followed her around everywhere she went and watched over her. At night time after the sun had gone down, she and her family sat around the hot orange fire and had their dinner. Poppy noticed how the flames licked up towards the sky and the colors danced delicately over one another fading in and out. When it came time to go to bed, she changed out of the orange dress that made her look just like a little poppy flower.

The next morning Poppy woke up to the rooster crowing. Her eyes flew open and she wondered if she missed the sunrise. She sat up and looked around. All she could see was grey and black and white, everywhere. She looked outside and the sky was full of grey streaks. "Well, I must be dreaming!" she thought to herself and fell back to sleep. Her dreams were full of rainbows and sunsets and fields of flowers. She woke up again to her mother banging on the door for her to wake up and come down to breakfast, but when she opened her eyes, everything was grey again. Poppy had no idea what was happening and was frightened. Was something wrong with her? She jumped out of bed and stumbled downstairs to the kitchen. "Mother, mother, I cannot see colors today! What's wrong with me?" She cried.

"What are you talking about Poppy? Slow down!" Her mother said.

"I woke up this morning and I couldn't see color, only grey and white and black!" She told her earnestly. Her mother looked at her with bewilderment.

"Why, you have quite an imagination, my child. What are these things you are talking about? Grie and corlor and..and black, what are these, imaginary friends?"

"They are colors mother, colors!"" Poppy couldn't think how to explain what colors were. She was so dreadfully confused about how her mother had forgotten what colors were.

"Well if you don't want to tell me that's okay, just wash your hands and take your place at the table. I made you some bacon and eggs." Poppy washed her hands and took her seat at the table but couldn't see the red-brown of the bacon or the bright yellow yolk. She tried to explain this to her mother but came up short. How could you explain color to someone who doesn't know what it is? Poppy hurriedly ate breakfast and ran outside. Everything there was different shades of grey. Her orange tabby Milo came padding up to her and she saw that his coat was grey too. Poppy bent down and looked into his usually wild green eyes, seeing only a dull grey. Throughout the day Poppy questioned everyone she saw about "color" and they had no clue what she was talking about. Poppy got very upset because no one seemed to understand her and she missed the colors so dearly. Did she just imagine color? Did she just make it up?

That night Poppy dreamed again of the most vibrant colors. There were rainbow rivers and autumn leaves and blue skies. Poppy woke up to the cry of the rooster and it was all gone. She went back to her grey and colorless life. She never saw color anymore, except when she was asleep and dreaming. Soon she stopped dreaming. She grew old and forgot all about color.

One day when Poppy was getting on in her years she was outside watching her granddaughter. Her granddaughter tried to tell her about a strange dream she had the night before. She couldn't describe it to Poppy, everything just looked different, and bright, very very bright. Suddenly, a memory was awakened in Poppy's mind, one that was long forgotten and buried deep. A memory of color. All of a sudden, bright yellow burst from the sun and fell to the earth in golden beams. From the top of the sky, the color blue slowly gushed down to the horizon like a waterfall. The blades of grass beneath her feet erupted in green hues. Her eyes landed on the big red barn, now faded pink with age. She then looked at her granddaughter who she saw had bright orange hair. Poppy found her eyes, they were the wildest green, just like her old tabby cat Milo.

Imaginary Monster

By Sophia Ospina (Finalist)

The breeze blows softly through the trees of Scofield Dr. It's the middle of summer and it's over 90 degrees, so you take refuge under the shade of a magnificent, 80-foot-tall southern magnolia tree. The grass is soft and lush in the front of the house, and the backyard is filled with toys and things to keep the children of the household entertained. There is a tire swing that hangs loosely to the colossal tree. To one side of the tree, there is an array of grapefruit and lemon trees surrounded by an assortment of picture-perfect rocks, seeming fake as they create a boundary between the grass and trees. On the other side, lies a patio with weather-faded matching chairs and sofas that are flooded with pillows. Also, present on the cement patio is a clay chiminea, characterized by its burnt rim. Parallel to the patio is an array of rosemary bushes and a half-broken, faded brown picket fence that leads to another patio. This smaller, brick-floored area contains a dusty grill and an overgrown lemon tree with wood chips surrounding its base.

Two children emerge from the one-story Spanish-style home. A young boy, around the age of 6, and a bubbly 10-year-old girl frolic around the uneven terrain of the backyard. They play various games of tag and hide and seek in the bushes. In one particular game of hide and seek, the girl discovers a loose tile in the picket fence that separates her house from the expansive backyard of her neighbor. She easily slips her small and elastic limbs through the brown fence and reaches the new planet of a new patio. The backyard is right next to hers, yet so different. Compared to her clean, green, and friendly backyard this one seems to be much darker. The fallen leaves from her massive tree also settle into this backyard, creating almost an entire floor of southern magnolia leaves. She can't go far without the piles under her feel collapsing. The little boy spends almost 15 minutes trying to find her and eventually yells a sign of surrender and she emerges from the distinct crawlspace. They hear their mother call them in for lunch and race each other inside.

Then there's me. I am the security they always refuge in. I am their solace, their home within their home. Obviously, their mother doesn't know about me, if she did, I think she'd lose her mind. Same with their father, who always seems to be busy at work. Poor fellow doesn't know he's ruining his life. That's beside the point. As they run inside, tripping over themselves without care, they know I'll still be there once they return from filling their stomachs with peanut butter and jelly. Such a delectable meal. Screams of delight and munching at food can be distinguished from a mile away.

I'm stalling. It's time to introduce myself in a less ominous way because to put it plainly I'm simply their imaginary friend. However, I am no plain-faced creature like you imagine, I am deadly. Imagine the more gruesome fantasy that you can conjure up in your minuscule brain. Done? Perfect, now multiply that by 3 million. That's me. My four legs lead up to my muscular body covered in jet black fur, that has cracks filled with sparks of magma as if I were being constantly broken and restored by the devil himself. My massive tail is a destructor within itself. My sharp snout leads solely to my bone-shattering jaw and jarring teeth. My final distinctive feature is my eyes, sharp glowing orbs of explosive fire.

I do however have a soft spot for the little ones. They always find a way to make me melt or at least more than I already do. To them, I'm just a big puppy dog that glows, and I'm fine with that, as long as I can bring them comfort and security as they develop a sense of their surroundings and the cruel world they live in. My job is to be a leader, guiding them through their fragile adolescence which I fear will be coming to an end soon. I can't stay with them after the age of 11, don't ask me why because I don't know, it's just the rules. Familiar screams and giggles escape the crack of the backdoor, which means my pups are back out to play.

The thick air of freedom and fulfillment easily flows in and out of our lungs as the adrenaline of youth surges through our veins. This is happiness in its truest, purest form. I know I have to leave them soon and it shatters me into trillions of pieces because I know for a fact that I have never and will never love someone as much as I love these two. Their grimey fingers and toes after digging up worms for me, their smiles dripping with ice cream freshly melted by the summer sun, their wonder at the excitement of the world around them, their ability to conjure up anything in the blink of an eye using solely their imaginations, but most of all, I'll miss how effortlessly and unconditionally they have loved me, despite the fact that I look like I could tear them to shreds. I think this is my awe at their bravery in entrusting me to not only be their best friend but their mentor and biggest supporter. I am their imaginary friend, but despite the name, our love and companionship are nothing near imaginary. And that my friends, is what it feels like to be your imaginary friend.

Lured

By Abbi Payne (Finalist and Honorable Mention)

Moonlight bathed the world in an ethereal glow. The wind whispered careless nothings to emerald leaves, its call finding the ears of a small girl.

She was curled up on her side, limbs tangled in blankets as she tossed and turned. The moon neared its zenith, and the child had yet to close her eyes. Should she wake her parents? No, that would make it the fourth time this week. But she was scared, and aren't parents supposed to comfort their children?

When the wind's words drifted into her ears, she jumped at the opportunity for adventure. She barely paused to grab her coat before tramping outside.

The grass ticked her ankles; the trees closest appeared to beckon her. She stopped when she saw its dark cervices and shadowy trails. The girl remembered her mother's warnings. She didn't want to see the disappointment in her eyes, hear the fear in her voice.

Just as she turned her back, the wind grabbed onto her hat,

flinging it into the woods. A soft cry escaped her lips as her beloved hat disappeared.

Well, now she had to retrieve it.

She stepped into the woods, cringing away from branches when they dipped too close. The moon was her only friend, lighting her path with pale little specks. She shoved her hands in her pockets, trying not to imagine what creatures might lurk in the dark pockets of the trees, in the dens near their roots.

The woods seemed to breathe. She suddenly remembered the stories her brothers told to scare her. ""Don't go into the woods at night,"" they'd warned. ""The Folk might grab you."" She held her breath, waiting for something vicious to come and drag her way.

No. Those are just stories. That's what her mother said when she caught the boys. They were telling her nonsense to scare her. That's right. She steeled herself and resumed her search.

The woods came to life. No longer did the shadows to her back reign supreme. Mushrooms popped up along her path: red-spotted white, mottled brown, speckled gray, swirls of purple. She was surrounded by dew on silky flowers and a steady drip of golden honey. The trees grew at odd angles here, crooked but elegant. And the world hummed. With life, with magic—she didn't know.

Soon, she happened upon a small creek, chirping and babbling, lost in its thoughts. The girl had forgotten her lost hat, enraptured with the beauty that surrounded her. Little did she know, she should have heeded her brother's stories. Little did she know, there was a reason her mother didn't want her out after dark.

Oblivious, the girl hopped across the creek, congratulating herself on her cautiousness. Yet, she didn't notice the eyes that had gathered to watch her—hidden amongst the trees, cloaked in shadows.

She carried on, admiring a gold mushroom. So caught up by its sparkle, she tripped. For a moment the illusion seemed to falter, viscous darkness closing in—

She stood and dusted herself off. The woods were just as they'd been before. But now, there was a sickly sweetness to them. A wrongness she couldn't place. The colors too bright, the creek too blue. Even the air seemed too thick. It smelled of flowers and honey and all sorts of wonderful things, but it was too strong, too cloying. ""That's how the Folk get you,"" her brothers had leered, mischievous grins on their faces.

She turned on her heels and ran.

Something rumbled to life, hot on her heels. The child screamed. Legs pumping, heart racing. What were once beautiful branches turned to terrible talons, snapping at her skirt and scratching her cheeks. Gorgeous flowers tugged on her shoes, and she tumbled down the hill.

The thing was still behind her; there was no escape. Tears welled in her eyes as she cried for her mother, her brothers, anyone. She tensed, preparing for the worst.

But the woods were silent, holding their breath.

Instead of a monster, a young man stepped out of the

trees. His brow furrowed with concern. "What happened to you?" His voice was gentle as he approached, kneeling down to her level.

She sniffled, wiping her nose on her sleeve. "I– I–" She began. Her cheeks stung, her dress was in tatters, and blood crept down her arm. All this over a hat. Tears spilled over, her breaths mere gasps.

"It's alright…" He ripped a piece of fabric off his cloak, holding it up to her. "May I?" She nodded. "Shh… it's alright." He wrapped the strip of fabric around her cut. "There. Now, where are your parents?"

The child took a look around the woods. These trees were unfamiliar, and there was no sign of home. "I… I don't know. I'm sorry…"

"It's nothing to apologize for," said the man, standing. He held himself in the sure way only adults could, but he looked barely older than twenty. "What's your name?"

And like a fool, she gave it to him.

He smiled again, but she didn't notice the little twinkle in his eye, the satisfaction in his gait as they stepped onto a path. She was never so glad to see packed dirt, the promise of her boring old house. She thanked him, remembering that it was kind to do so.

It was her second mistake.

"Before you go," he said. "I believe you have a debt to cash in."

It was only then she registered his tapered ears, his sharp smile, and his ageless face. It was only then she realized. Names have power; thank yous are binding, especially to one of them. It was too late. The monster had been next to her all along.

"No," she pleaded, "You can't–"

He shrugged as if she were nothing but an ant under his shoe or a bug that had flown too close. "Didn't your parents ever tell you? It's not safe for children in the woods." He leaned in. "Something might come along to get them."

Miracles for Mateo

By Clara Wiggins (Finalist)

I carry the fabric of my ten pound dress in clenched fists as my feet hit the pavement, bare and tired. My hair whips and bounces over my shoulders and into my face. The church doors are mere meters away.

I couldn't think twice about my streaming tears as I barge the doors open and let the words rip from my throat, ""I object!"" before collapsing to my knees on the floor.

When I bring my face back up to the audience, there isn't one familiar face. But all of them look down at me in shock and horror. There's a deafening silence before a shriek rings through the pews. Suddenly I'm no longer the center of attention as everyone's heads turn to the open casket and the body thats hand is curling around the edge.

""What?"" I mutter to myself as I crawl on my palms and knees to a seat so I can catch my breath. The reality sets in that I've crashed a rather elaborate funeral—and I've apparently woke the dead.

•••

What was one to bring to the resurrection of a dead man? I hadn't a clue so I'd brought a dozen roses and a box of chocolates. post-Valentine's day sales are impossible to pass up.

I climbed up the smoothed white staircase. I wasn't cultured enough to know if it was marble or quartz. Whatever it was, it looked expensive. I knocked on the door and waited maybe half a minute before it was answered and I was led in by an older male. he had chiseled facial features and his eyes looked ageless.

I'd gotten the call this morning—a week after the incident—that the guy from the funeral was fully recovered. He'd been in some devastating car accident, something truly awful. His friend in the car was left completely severed in half from the impact. It was something out of a horror movie and I couldn't clear my search history fast enough as I looked at the news images from it.

""Ellie, is it?"" The male said as he placed his palm on my upper back to guide me past the foyer and to a study room.

""Yes. And you are Mr. Drake?"" I replied.

""Correct. Mateo will be right with you. He's been pretty adamant about meeting you."" He left me awkwardly in the room, chocolate in one hand and flowers in the other. There was a small table with a vase that I could put the roses in but the tulips in it would need to be removed. As I contemplated whether to act on the impulse of dumping the tulips, the door from which I came creaked open.

I turned around and sucked in a sharp breath. It was partly out of fear but mostly from surprise.

""Mateo."" he said, giving me a slow blink and nod, but thankfully not giving me the embarrassment of having to shake his hand.

""Ellie."" I responded and shifted uncomfortably, hoping he'd take the hint of my full hands and relieve me of the strain. He ungracefully pulled the tulips from the crystal vase, shook the stems dry and reached out for the roses. He placed those in the vase and behind the door, he discarded the tulips to a small trash bin and returned to our competitive gaze.

""I want to thank you."" He spoke smoothly as he unbuttoned his dress shirt sleeves and rolled them. ""But I can't.""

""What?"" My eyebrows furrowed as I slid the chocolates to the mini-table and left my fingers tapping across it.

""You brought me back to life."" He shrugged.

""It was a mere coincidence I'm sure.""

""I didn't want to be alive.""

""Oh."" My tapping stopped and I folded my arms to my waist. He paced around the table until it stood between us and he continued to gaze upon me.

""Why'd you do it?"" He spat, his voice teetering on the edge of anger. I stood back as I realized he was growing hostile towards me.

""Believe me, I had absolutely no clue there was a funeral

going on when I arrived at the church. I was expecting a wedding but I was much too late."" I mentally sighed at the ending I'd truly wanted for that day. He reached for the chocolates at the same time as I. He immediately retracted but not before I felt the cold touch of his palm.

We spoke the opposite sentences in perfect unison: ""You're so cold."" and ""You're so warm.""

""Why'd you bring food?"" He said at a near chuckle but still trying to maintain his demanding demeanor. I took advantage of the playful side he was letting slip out.

""Well I'm sorry, I didn't know what dead people like to eat."" I smile unevenly and moved back to the table.

""You're a comic. You're very...human."" Mateo's hands slipped to his pockets and he stood back cooly. ""What do you actually eat on this side of town? The caribou population is quite overgrown.""

""Oh, I was raised partly vegetarian. I've never had meat."" I replied honestly.

""God, I don't mean meat, I mean blo—"" His words stopped and he tilted his head in confusion. I mirrored his actions until he dryly opened and closed his mouth.

""You're staring."" I said as the silence was growing awkward. I was uncomfortable as he kept staring.

""You don't know, do you?"" His brows were coming together to create a face that mimicked one in pain.

"Ellie, you're a vampire."

Not All Heroes Wear Capes

By Natalie Rice (Finalist)

"Hey Ben, look."

"I see,"" the voice snickered and there was silence save for their soft footfalls. They were a long way down the block, but had already picked their target.

The woman tapped her way through the bustle of afternoon foot traffic. She flicked her wrist deftly, detecting each bump in the sidewalk with her cane. She had walked this route a dozen, no a hundred times. And each day it fascinated her how different and similar it could be to the day before.

"Watch this," Ben hissed.

Using the cane to guide herself down the street was second nature to the woman by now. While she moved, she twitched a finger in time with each passing second.

Shhwap. Something clattered and bounced along the

cement. It sounded like her cane.

The woman's finger twitched. 1, 2, 3, 4. . .

Her cane knocked against something hollow and she ducked around it. A moment later, her hand brushed against a jacket. And the side of someone's bag.

. . . 89, 90, 91, 92 . . .

Around her, the world was silent. There was no crinkling of fabric, no laughter, no voices, and no rumble of cars. She had been deaf and blind since the age of twelve, due to an automobile accident. However, her disability had come with an added quirk.

. . . 212, 213, 214, 215 . . .

Her fingers kept tapping in time with the big hand on a clock.

. . . 296, 297, 298, 299 . . .

The woman whipped her cane up away from the cement. There was no sound, only the vertebration of a body striking concrete. A sweet perfume tickled the woman's nose. A passerby had stopped to gawk at something.

The woman set her cane down. It nudged against a soft body, who she assumed was Ben. He had missed his target. The perfume wafted away as the woman moved on. She used her cane as a guide and listened carefully as she continued on.

"No! No, please. I didn't see anything." This voice was sobbing. It was young, innocent, and honest.

"As if we'd believe that."

BAM!

The woman startled, but her fingers were already tapping. 1, 2, 3, 4 . . .

"Look."

"She's blind and probably deaf."

"I don't care."

BAM!

She only reached 20 when she realized something was wrong.

It was completely silent. No more shuffling, no more voices, no more sound.

All the noise was completely gone. Her hearing . . . it was like she was truly deaf.

The woman knew no world was this quiet. It wasn't possible. She should have been able to hear incoming people, traffic she would cross, or at least something. But all was silent. It shouldn't have been possible.

Unless. . .

The woman halted. Someone crashed into her before they skirted around her and kept moving. A dog knocked into her knees and tickled her calf with its soft breaths.

Someone's shoulder caught hers and nearly sent her tumbling to the ground. The woman stood still for one heartbeat more before she was off. She moved fast, her cane catching in every crack of the sidewalk. Sometimes her feet outran her cane, but she didn't care. She had somewhere to be.

. . . 134, 135, 136, 137 . . .

Her cane hit the bumps at the edge of the sidewalk and for the first time in her entire life, she charged across the intersection without pause. She felt a vehicle whoosh past her body and flutter her clothes in its wind. Her cane hit a pothole, but it was a minor distraction.

Caution had been flung into the wind.

. . . 203, 204, 205, 206 . . .

She rounded another corner and her nose alerted her to the scents of gasoline, men, and fear.

. . . 278, 279, 280, 281 . . .

The woman was almost running now. Her nose had caught another whiff of sweat and cheap deodorant. She couldn't hear or see a thing, but she knew what had to happen.

. . . 296, 297, 298, 299 . .

Her hand caught the edge of rough sleeve and she shoved as hard as she could. She felt the heat of a bullet sear past her face.

BAM!

And the second one hit her chest.

BAM!

Then all was dark.

. . .

The woman came to slowly. She could not see or hear, but she gradually became aware of cool bedsheets and a warm room. Something chemical tasting lingered on the back of her tongue.

"How could she have possibly known?" Someone wondered. "She's blind and deaf." The woman relaxed and her mouth twitched. Automatically, her fingers started tapping.

"I don't know."

"It's a miracle."

"That girl is alive because of her. Those men would have robbed and then likely killed her."

When the woman heard those words, she relaxed fully. Though she was still tapping, still waiting for the voices to speak in real time, she was filled with elation. The words took several moments to truly process, but once they did, she felt her lips curve into a smile.

And she couldn't have been more happy.

Reaper

By Presley Roose (Finalist)

This is it, I'm at the end of my life. My jaunty lifestyle is coming to an end and I'm just waiting to be ravaged by death himself.

□□□

My last thoughts before I was dragged to the other side of life. Oh how wrong my doctrine was. Yes, he was haggard - absolutely in rags - but he was in no way predatory. His voice was low, but soft and almost comforting. If I wasn't looking into the lifeless eyes of my recently deceased body I would have thought his voice to be charming. It was exotic, with an accent I had never heard before in my life.

"Come with me Axel, we have somewhere we need to go," was the first thing he said to me before he grabbed my shoulder firmly and led me away.

"You, Axel, were no angel. But the old man wants you upstairs," he chuckled as he let go of my shoulder and allowed me to fleet my eyes across the new surroundings.

"So, uh, why didn't you take me straight there?" I questioned.

"You humans really do attribute death with immediate results, don't you?" he cocked an eyebrow but it was not belittling in any way, it was humorous, "Anyway, I didn't take you there because since the beginning of time there have always been forces that try to prevent the passing of souls, and I'm the one that has to parry them off and lead you to where you need to be."

"Forces?" I asked, "What kind of forces?"

"The bad ones, the ones you don't want to mess with, the ones that will rip you to shreds, the ones that are turncoats to our father."

"Oh," I murmured.

"But don't be afraid, there has never been an instance since I have been put in this position where I was unable to guide a soul through." he confidently told me as he began to move forward and motioned for me to follow.

I sighed with relief and continued after him. He seemed menial but trustworthy. We were climbing upwards, on what seemed to be an overhang.

"This is where it's going to get difficult, but don't let your faith in me waiver, I won't let you go."

I didn't understand what he meant until we reached the peak, where he wrapped his arms around me just before jumping off. We didn't reach the bottom of the drop for what seemed to be an eternity. But when we did, I noticed something new in my pocket and reached down to see what it was; a note.

"Heaven is on the other side of this wallow, follow my directions and you're going to make it."

When I raised my head to show him, he was gone, and I was left to fend for myself in purgatory.

The Artificer

By Mason Gabriel George (Finalist)

In the center of the town sat a stone tower. The tower held but one room at its top. For now, this room sat empty and organized, the light of the late afternoon sun fell lazily through the curtains, catching the dust as it danced through the air. This is the workshop of the Artificer, a maker of magic. He imbues the ordinary within the weave of magic to create extraordinary artifacts of great power. His room is full of exotic components and tools. The floor is bare wood and only a single lantern hangs from the ceiling. His workbench has numerous shelves, some filled to the brim with nearly identical pencils, others held carefully sealed containers of multicolored ink that seemed to swirl in the light. Atop his workbench a sheet of leather concealed an assortment of woodcarver's tools, small pots, and numerous empty bottles. Across the room stood bookcases stocked with jars of preserved components, animal parts in jars, crystals, and spices from around the world. Next to this bookcase sat an open chest of empty scrolls and paper. Ascending footsteps approach, the door flies open and the

Artificer enters his workshop. In his hand he carries a new design, a new job. He has been commissioned by a wealthy and influential bard to create an instrument capable of focusing magic into song. He must work carefully to fit the meticulous design; failure could mean more than lost income when you work with magic after all. Magic is a weave of energy, a web of power that connects everything since the moment of creation. Every object is a vessel, a container for magic to fill. The Artificer's work is dangerous for he must take a container and make it draw in more magic. For now, he starts simple, completing the vessel so the magic could fill it. He takes his carving tools and grabs from the woodpile, taking the shape of the instrument from the log. He finishes as the sun begins to set, he snaps his hands and the lantern lights, once more brightening up the workshop. He stands, donning the goggles and gloves as he walks to the bookshelf. He carefully grabs multiple jars and sets them on his work bench, stashing a few in drawers. Caution is important now; he cannot afford to make any mistakes. Carefully he mixes the biological components, making a wax for the instrument so it would be able to direct magic more efficiently. A wind stirs around his room, the lantern shaking on its chain, flickering. As he applies the wax the wind picks up, threatening to smear his work. The wood carving tools fall to the floor and scatter around the room as the wind picks up. As he works thunder crashes through the room, shaking his workbench and his shelves, a jar tumbling to the floor where it shattered. He raises three fingers and chants as he slowly makes a circle with his hand in the air. A wire lifts into the air held aloft gently by a spectral hand. The wire begins to heat till glowing before the hand gently stretches it ultrathin and carefully attaches it to the neck of the instrument. As the wire cools the heat fills the room, soon the tower top begins to feel like a molten forge. The cold swirling wind picks up the heat and suddenly the room spins into a storm around him, clouds as dark and as deadly as the night fill the ceiling above the Artificer. He feels a cold drop of water on the back of his neck as he unfurls his workbenches' water proof cover over the instrument. He could not get it wet right now; it would become unstable. He works beneath the tarp as the storm's rage grows around him, a small bolt lightning strikes the shelves, igniting them. He stops for a moment, gently whispering an incantation. The fire is instantly snuffed as water suddenly appears in a torrent above it. As he finishes the wax, he reaches for a jar, the instant his hand grips it thunderous waves of crashing noise burst within his room, shattering the window, the bottles left out, and the jar he holds all in one fell swoop. Calmly he reaches into a low drawer in his workbench and brings out another, he would have to replace the bottles and window later but for now he must continue, he could not risk failure. The storm spins into a frenzy, throwing anything not secured. The Artificer works quickly, grinding and mixing components before gently applying them to the instrument. He stands, fighting the wind as he grabs a crystal off of the shelf. In the eye of the storm, he meticulously carves it into spiraling shapes so each would fit perfectly in place on his instrument. Stumbling back to his workbench he is battered by papers the storm whips around his room, nearly dropping the perfectly carved crystals. As he carefully puts each crystal into place the wind begins to slow, the clouds to dissipate, the heat to fade. With the final crystal in place only a light breeze stirs his room. He looks through the broken window and sees the sun begin to rise. Good, he had finished just on time. Carefully lifting his creation, he feels the wind stir his hair gently, he walks to the door, stepping through, he would clean up later. He exits his tower, making his way back to his shop to meet the client, this would fetch a high price indeed. A powerful instrument for a powerful customer. A smile stretches his face as he crosses the calm town, few were stirring in the market at this hour but those who were there made way for him. The instrument catches the light of the sun and seems to glow with it, the wind blowing only around him.

The Toy Soldier

By Julia Bobe (Finalist)

Once, there was a toy soldier. He stood proudly on a deck of cards with his bandit. The soldier was owned by a collector, who cherished him as his prize. This was because the soldier was the most expensive, and it was the only gift that the collector could give to his daughter for ten birthdays. The soldier had a fine coat, and was painted so beautifully. The soldier stayed on the daughter's desk with the deck of cards.

There was one thing that made this toy soldier unique. It had a soul. The soldier didn't know why he had a soul. But he was used to it, despite it making him fully conscious about being a lifeless toy. The soldier never experienced the joys of running around or laughing with friends. He couldn't quite comprehend those things.

The only thing he longed for was the collector's daughter.

She was a young beautiful woman with personality. She cared so much for her father and read many classics of Shakespeare and Greek mythology. The daughter even talked to herself near the soldier because of her confidence. She was the perfect woman to the soldier. The daughter was the only thing that tormented the soldier's forever frozen body.

One day, the collector was so poor that he decided to sell the toy soldier, despite the daughter's pleas and promised to give her a better toy soldier. The soldier realized this over a conversation in the room he was in, and wept silently. Wept that he would soon leave the daughter's presence, never to see her beautiful face and intelligent voice ever again. The only comfort he could hear was that there was no other toy soldier that could replace him in the daughter's heart, as he had the value of being the one thing from her childhood. As he was nothing more than a toy, the soldier could only pray that he could be with the daughter forever.

The soldier's prayers were answered. From heaven, a fairy came down to the soldier's with the sunrise. Her hair was as fine as silk, and her skin was as pure as the milk. The fairy came down as a messenger of God. The soldier was frightened by her appearance, but she told him not to worry. He was about to receive everything he prayed for.

The fairy makes a deal with the soldier. The soldier will become a human that he can be with the collector's daughter. The soldier however, will have three days to win a card game, and if he's unable to play or loses, he will turn back into a toy, forever tormented by his lost freedom. The soldier considers the deal extreme, but it is only chance to be with the daughter. So the soldier agrees, promising that he will win a card game to be a human forever. The fairy then grants him his wish.

The toy soldier feels his body change. He becomes larger and more organic, finally able to close his eyes. When the soldier wakes up, he is outside the house of the collector. Despite the cold, the soldier is delighted by his movements he can now make. He expresses his feelings through funny faces in the reflection of a window and moves his body freely through the snow. The only problem for the soldier was his own clumsiness, but that was nothing compared to the new bodily freedom he felt throughout.

As fun as it was to be a human for him, the soldier was getting cold and needed shelter. He knocked on the collector's door, which was answered by the collector's daughter. She agreed to let him in. As she prepared, the daughter talked to the soldier, interested in his handsomeness and great understanding for her interests. She wondered why the soldier looked so much like her toy, especially with him seemingly trying to hide the reason he knew so much about literature, but the thought never passed as a pure coincidence.

Wanting to be with the soldier more, the collector's daughter asked if he could come to a friend's house for Mouche. The daughter admitted that she could rarely play it because she never had that many friends. The soldier was overjoyed at this opportunity. It was the card game he needed to become a human. Though the soldier had to hold back his joy to look less suspicious. The daughter was delighted that he could play.

The soldier and the collector's daughter arrived at the friend's house to play Mouche. When the game is about to begin, the soldier notices that everyone seems really irritated that he has no money to give. Throughout the game, losers have to give up the money that they have. The soldier then realized that everyone playing was gambling, including the collector's daughter. It was impossible for the soldier that an honest and sensible woman like the daughter would ever gamble. But the soldier kept on playing.

Eventually all the other players lost the game. It was only the collector's daughter and the soldier who were playing. The soldier was terrified by the thought of beating the love of his life just to be human. The soldier tried to have a witty conversation with the daughter to ignore the dreaded thought. The daughter could go along with the soldier's games just fine, but it still couldn't quiet his mind.

As the collector's daughter and soldier play, the soldier's biggest dream and worst fear come true. He could deal with the highest and lowest trump card, which would give him the greatest card-points. He could win right there and become the human forever, winning the collector's daughter's heart. But then she would gamble away all her money. The collector was so poor, that he would likely beat her. Could the daughter even love the soldier?

So the soldier doesn't play his cards. He waits patiently for the collector's daughter to find her own trump cards. A few minutes later, she gets her highest and lowest trump cards. The daughter is relieved as she wins, along with the soldier. She is given dozens of euros as the soldier is ready to leave, ready to leave his freedom behind. The daughter finds the soldier's behavior strange, but he leaves before she can ask.

The soldier goes back near the collector's home to turn back into a toy. His body shrinks and stiffens as he loses all control he once had. Becoming nothing more than plastic on the streets. The soldier mourns with his last tears the day he had freedom. The day he could walk through the streets, laugh with the love of his life, and talk to people. It was the only day that the soldier could truly understand his own soul.

As the toy soldier was alone on the streets, the collector finds him after a long search. He picks up the soldier, appreciating the beauty of it. The collector gets ready to sell the soldier. He holds the soldier tightly, not ready to let go of it forever. The soldier was the only true beauty in the collector's possession, with a way to connect to the human heart. But the soldier was still worth enough to pay off debt.

But as the collector gets ready to go off and sell the soldier, his daughter comes running back. She is overjoyed by the money, failing to notice that her father had the toy soldier in his hand. When the daughter saw the soldier, she mourned and begged her father not to sell it as she had gotten enough money. The collector was upset when he learned how his daughter got the money, but she persisted that it was for their own good and that they have enough to not only pay off the debt, but to pay for valuables. The collector then decided to comply with his daughter's wishes and gave the toy soldier back to her. She happily took it back to her desk, laying it near her deck of cards.

The soldier also silently celebrated the joy that the collector's daughter felt as he stood motionless. His love for her was too strong for him to mourn his loss, as she was free. This love that the soldier felt for the daughter was strong enough to summon the fairy once again. The fairy couldn't grant the soldier the same wish again, but she could give him a chance to have his love for the daughter be spoken.

So she instead came to the collector's daughter. At first, the daughter was frightened by the fairy's appearance, but she assured her that she was a messenger of God. The fairy told the daughter that her toy soldier was in fact the man she invited to play Mouche with. Despite it sounding completely unreal, the daughter could believe it due to all the strange occurrences sorrowing the toy soldier. The fairy told the daughter that the toy soldier became human because of his soul and the love he had for her. When the daughter asked if the soldier could ever turn back into a human, the fairy replied "Only if you can love him back, not by his body's limitations, but by his soul.", before rising back into the heavens.

Trove of Imagination

By Lydia Cooper (Finalist and Honorable Mention)

"Onto the ship, me lady, or ye'll deal with me cutlass!" cried Ben, shoving his prisoner aboard in a splash of sea spray.

"Do we have to hold her for ransom again?" asked Jim. "Last time—"

"Don't question yer orders, cabin boy. I'm cap'n here, and I say she'll fetch lots of treasure."

"Yep," said Pearl cheerily. "It's exciting to be kidnapped by pirates. But your ship's a little small, isn't it?"

Ben strode across the deck, brandishing his cutlass, and scowled. "This here's the Stout Flamingo, terror of the seven seas! And if'n I hear ye criticizing Cap'n Barnacle Ben's vessel again, I'll make ye walk the plank meself."

"Myself," remarked Jim, beginning to steer the Stout Flamingo toward the rocky shore across the water.

"Ye'll be food for sharks too, Jim, if'n ye say another word about me English," snapped the captain.

Jim shrugged. Pearl stared around the pirate ship.

"What sea is this, Captain Ben?" she asked eagerly.

"I'm Cap'n Barnacle Ben—" the pirate began, but Jim broke in.

"This is the Stone Lagoon. I named it. We're going to hide our ship here until your relatives come and ransom you."

"Oh," said Pearl. "What's over there?" She pointed to the shore of the lagoon, spread with stony pools and puddles.

"That's the coast," Jim told her. "It's uninhabited, so we're going to bury our treasure there."

"Who's that on the shore, then?"

Ben said, "That's me parrot."

Pearl giggled. On the beach, so did the parrot.

Jim drew the ship up to the shore and jumped out, splashing through the puddles.

"Careful near the edge," said the parrot. "Don't slip."

Ben seized a large wooden chest from the deck and led Pearl off the ship too, skidding on the slick ground.

"Shh," hissed Jim. "Watch out near the water. This sea is full of sharks."

"I don't see any sharks," said Pearl.

"Well, where's your imagination?" returned Jim.

"Over here, Jim, to this sandy spot," called Ben, running across the stony shoreline to the beach, his footsteps going from sharp slap to dull thud. "Now dig the hole," he panted, "nice and deep, so me treasure's never found." He patted the chest fondly.

Jim waved a shovel and started to dig.

"I'll guard the prisoner," added Ben excitedly, grabbing Pearl's arm.

"Be gentle," scolded the parrot.

Ben let go of Pearl and said, "Want to see me treasure, landlubber?"

"Sure," said Pearl, bobbing on her toes. Ben opened the box with a clink.

"How's that?" he asked proudly. "Ahoy, Jim! Watch that shovel—yer getting sand in me treasure."

Pearl peered into Ben's sea chest. "Wow! I didn't know pirate treasure was like that. It looks like my bead necklaces."

Ben nodded and tapped his cutlass on the ground. "Shiver me timbers, Jim, are ye almost done?"

"Do you have to talk like that?" said Jim. "Yes—done." He stepped back from the deep hole in the beach.

"Aye, it be a good place for me treasure trove, matey," Ben

approved. "Yo-ho-ho!"

He dropped the battered chest into the hole with a dull thunk, and together the two pirates heaped it with sand.

"Back to me ship, then!" shouted Ben. "Onward, ye sea slugs!"

"Ben!" said the parrot. "Be polite."

Ben and Jim bounded back onto the Stout Flamingo, pulling Pearl after them.

"Run up the sails, Jim!" cried the captain.

"What sails?" asked Pearl, but Jim was sending the ship sweeping out to the deep end of the Stone Lagoon. The water bobbed under them, blue and a little green, spangled with dancing ribbons of light. Pearl leaned over the side and trailed her fingers through the waves.

"Ahoy!" yelled Ben. "Away from the edge, me lady, or the sharks'll get ye."

Pearl scuttled back. "What do sharks eat?"

"Everything," said Ben drearily.

"Hey, captain!" Jim called. "The wind's getting strong— want to help sail?"

Ben dashed promptly across the deck, waving his cutlass. "Storm at sea!" he shouted. "See those dark clouds? Shiver me timbers, we're in for a squall, matey!"

"I didn't mean to have a storm," Jim started, but Ben was

in full flow now.

"Gale's a blowing! Man the tiller or we'll capsize!"

Pearl jumped up. The ocean swelled suddenly high, and the Stout Flamingo bounced and dipped over the toppling waves. Lightning split the sky.

"The sharks are coming!" cried Jim. "See the fins?"

Dark, curving triangles appeared in the heaving water.

"Arr!" Ben roared. "Me good ship's sprung a leak!"

The Stout Flamingo shuddered. Then, in a wild flurry of boat and pirates and seawater, everything tumbled apart with a crash of spray.

"Don't splash so much," called the parrot from the shore.

"Me ship!" wailed Ben, surfacing with a splutter. "The sharks! We're all going to Davy Jones' Locker, shipmates!" He started to sink in a thrashing spasm of bubbles.

"That's enough, kids," said the parrot. "Are you ready for supper?"

And the sinking ship and pirates washed away, becoming three children clinging to a fat inflatable flamingo in a swimming pool.

"Oh, please, Mom," started Pearl, scrambling back onto the chubby flamingo with her wet hair sticking all over her face.

"Just five more minutes—"

"It was going to be fun to visit Davy Jones' Locker," said

Ben, pirate accent abandoned, and he reproachfully wiggled the pool noodle he'd used for a cutlass.

"No, it's getting dark," said their mother, who was perched in a deck chair. "Get out of the pool and dry off. You can keep playing another day."

Dripping, the three clambered out of the water and splashed across the slick concrete.

"Oh, and don't forget to take those beads out of the sandbox," added their mother as she passed them towels.

The children clattered off. In the water behind them, the flamingo bobbed, round and pink, plastic skin tight with air. There was still a glint of pirate treasure in the sandbox.

SECTION 2 – TRIALS

A Dream

By Jules Hau (Finalist)

A small girl. Standing alone. She stares upward. Toward the stars.

They shine brightly against the foreboding darkness. Beautiful hues, red, yellow, orange. How wondrous they are, far away above. How easy it must be, to only exist and shine. Oh, how we wish upon them, hoping for a miracle.

However, the girl knows.

Wishing upon a star will not make bad things disappear.

Wishing upon a star will not help you overcome a problem.

Wishing upon a star will not create a miracle.

Yet, she still wishes. She still hopes. Someday, one day, one week, one month, one year.

Something must happen. Someone must be able to help

her.

Oh stars, please give a sign.

A miracle.

"Vivi," A dividing light cuts through the darkness, outshining the stars. "Vivi, it's time to wake up." Something tugged at the girl, gently prodding her arm and head. "Viviane."

The girl awoke. She was in her room. Everything was where it was. The bed holding her was raised, allowing her to sit up. The pumps and tubes connected to her arm, pumping fluid from the IV stand. The curtains were drawn, making the room even smaller than it usually was.

Yes, this was where she was. In real life.

No stars shine out her window, the city skies hide them. The rhythmic beeping outside her open door, the same frequency over and over. The coming and going nurses in her room, giving her medication and food. The quiet hum that never leaves the girl, even in her dreams.

This was her life. At least, for now.

"Vivi, I'm checking your vitals okay?" Mandy, the girl's assigned nurse, stands at the end of the bed. He is wearing violet scrubs today, different from his blue scrubs from the day before.

It was a daily routine. Mandy wakes her up. Mandy checks vitals. Mandy leaves. A new nurse comes in. They check my IV levels. They give me food. They leave. Same schedule. Same day. Same week.

Yet, Mandy gives news.

News.

"Your mom is coming to see you, Vivi."

Her mother is a busy woman. She visits on occasion, nothing special when she enters the room. She talks with the nurses and staff, her daughter before going into deeper conversation with someone else.

The girl wonders what they talk about. Perhaps it is about her. Maybe about the weather. The girl is never quite sure. She has no time to think about it, as her mother enters her room a few moments later.

"Hey," Her mother cooed, making her way to the side of the bed. "How are you feeling?"

The girl told her mom she is doing well. Her mother can't help but smile.

"Well, how about we get out of here and take a little trip?" The girl stared blankly at her. Get out? Leave? As though having read her daughter's mind, the girl's mother reassured her, "Yes, honey. I'm taking you out of the hospital. The doctors said you can be discharged."

The girl nodded several times, pretending to understand what her mom had said. She was happy of course, getting out of this room. Her room. She could look around and see what is outside that door. This building. The girl was excited.

"Alright then, baby. Let's go to the car." She took the girl's hand and guided her out of the room.

The girl waved Mandy goodbye before walking next to her mom to the entrance of the hospital. They got into the car and drove onto the freeway. The girl stared out the window, seeing the hospital and city becoming a speck in the distance. She watched the roads become longer and bleak. However, overtime, the roads were covered with lush greenery. Bright, vibrant sunlight hitting the car windows and seats.

Her mom opened the windows, letting the cool breeze flush the girl's cheeks. She hadn't felt the breeze in so long. The girl was pleased.

The long, lush greens turned into sandy beaches and coastlines. Then to flowering fields and decadent trees. When her mother parked, they were standing on a plateau, looking out toward the sunset.

Everything was beautiful.

Everything was colorful.

Everything was more than anything the girl expected.

The girl was happy. Her mom hugged her tightly, giving her love and happy whispers.

"My baby. I'm so happy." Her mother had tears in her eyes. The girl was not sure why. Her mom looked happy but was shedding tears. Aren't tears for sad memories? She listened to her mother's rambles and tears.

"...Vivi." A distant voice called. However, the girl did not take her eyes from her mother. Her mom was hugging her. Giving time to see her. Took her on a trip to such pretty sights.

"Vivi..." But the girl shook her head. She wanted to stay here. She didn't want to go.

"Viviane."

The girl opens her eyes. Mandy is standing in the room, wearing green scrubs. He is going to check vitals. The girl looks around. She could not stop tears from flowing.

The girl knew.

Yet she still hopes.

In her dreams.

Faith Can Stop a Bullet

By Bryson Bentley (Finalist)

Have you ever thought of what it would be like to fight in a war? Well, my grandpa knew, he fought in World War II. In fact, his stories are known by many. During WWII he was given many nicknames, but the name I want to talk about is "Dead-eye-Dick." My Grandpa was in SaarBirg, Germany on December 23rd, 1944 in an empty town, which was covered in snow, by the Saarbirg River when a miracle took place. He was in a house with two other men named Paul and Herman to watch for German action when two Germans entered the town and started checking the houses. Arriving at the house my grandpa and his two buddies were hiding in, the Germans opened the door to find Paul pointing his gun at them. "Hande Hoch (Hands Up)," he yelled to the Germans. One dropped his gun, but the other started to raise his rifle at Paul, so my grandpa, who was in the attic with Herman, shot him. Immediately the other German took off running through the snow. " Halt, Halt," Paul cried as he watched the man run.

Since the man knew which house they were in, my grandpa

didn't want to let the guy make it back across the bridge. My grandpa raised his carbine and fired a shot right between the German's shoulders; he kept running. My grandpa fired again. This time he fell forward into the snow, which was several inches deep, but then jumped back up and kept running. In fact, he seemed to run even faster. My grandpa picked up Herman's M1 rifle because the man was now too far for his carbine to reach. Three more times my grandpa shot him in the back, but he kept running, then, right before the bridge, he turned and sprinted behind a house. "Where did that other one go?" Paul asked from the street. "I don't know," my grandpa replied, "but wherever he is, he should have five holes in the middle of his back." My grandpa was confused because5 he had qualified as an "expert" on both guns. My grandpa thought the sights must be out of adjustments on both guns but then he aimed at an ornament on top of a light pole about fifty yards away and hit it "dead center."

In the end, they found the guy who was shot and brought him back to the house and was able to, with the help of an interpreter, question him. It was interesting4 that they had found him kneeling in the snow praying, so they thought my grandpa must know him. After a while of questioning, they asked him if he was praying that they wouldn't kill him. He said "Ach nein," meaning "no." He explained that he prayed for that blessing before he crossed the bridge, and when they found him praying, he was "thanking God-in-Heaven" that He had saved him. My grandpa inspected his back and surprisingly the only marks from his shots were a bullet hole in his sleeve, the others had missed completely. When my grandpa was done inspecting, the interpreter turned to him and said " Hey, Hall, aren't you Mormon?" "Yeah he is," replied one of the men. They discovered that a missionary that my Grandpa knew from Arizona had baptized the man who had prayed. One of the men told the German that he was lucky that he wasn't killed because," Hall is Dead-eye-Dick, a cowboy from Arizona." This story shows how not even an expert gunman with the nickname of "Dead-eye-Dick" is more powerful than a prayer of faith.

GET COMFORTABLE WITH BEING UNCOMFORTABLE

By Lance Mathis (Finalist)

At halftime during a game my sophomore year, the head football coach said, "Get comfortable with being uncomfortable," We were playing against our main rivals. We were down by 14 at half, with the worst conditions any of us had ever experienced. It was about 30 degrees and an absolute monsoon. It poured down rain the whole game, and the weather affected us so badly because we were a passing team who does not excel at running the football. That quote could not have been said any better. As quarterback, I knew something had to be done in the second half. In the second half we played better, but we were still unable to pull off the win. This quote really stuck with me, not only through football, but through life as well.

This quote has become my guiding principle. For example, when I am at a pep rally, and they ask me to speak, if I am scared to talk to someone, or even in football games. If I go up there scared and not wanting to do the speech, I will more than likely embarrass myself and look stupid, but if I go up there telling myself to get comfortable with the speech, I will no doubt embrace the challenge of going up and talking in front of a ton of people and will not look as bad as I was going to look before. It is a mindset. A person tells themselves when uncomfortable to get used to it and go ahead and get comfortable doing whatever it is they are doing. Most people can relate to this feeling, and I am so thankful I have a coach that has taught me more than just football skills. He has taught me how to handle life in general, be a better person, son, brother, friend, and student. Life is going to be hard and having learned certain ways to handle difficult situations I know will come in handy for sure. I just hope I can build on what I have learned to be the best person I can be. College is going to be very challenging, I can appreciate the challenge and just hope to apply the skills my family, coaches, teachers and even my friends have taught me over time.

In many situations people need this mindset. If a person has that confidence in himself, he can accomplish way more than he even thought possible. Another instance where someone might say this quote to herself would be if she wants to ask someone out, but she does not have the nerve to do it or if she is just plain and simply scared. She just has to tell herself to get comfortable being uncomfortable. Go ask the person out. She will learn to be comfortable doing things that make her feel uncomfortable. Can you imagine the amount of opportunities that have been missed by people just being scared they will be rejected or look dumb?

A lot of growth can come from this mindset. I can

become the most confident version of myself. It is actually pretty simple. In life is where this quote mainly translates, but also on the football field as well. When it was really cold last year against Atoka, I had to tell myself the quote a lot, and it helped me. Anyone who has ever been to a football game late in a season, will know just how cold it is. It gets stinkin miserable out there. But I just have to have a really good mindset and attitude about it and I will always play very well. I hate playing late in the season, like weeks 6-10, it starts to get really cold, and it gets below freezing a lot of nights. That is why when it starts getting cold, I start going outside a lot more to get used to the weather. I go hunting a lot anyway so that helps me out a lot, but I will go outside in 35 degrees Fahrenheit in just shorts, no socks, shoes or t-shirt, just me and my shorts. It is a really satisfying feeling knowing that I am getting used to the cold weather. I can just tell. Even when I go to team breakfast in the mornings when it is below freezing, I drive to the church, (or wherever we are planning to eat breakfast) with the windows on my truck down. At the time it sucks, sure. But if I just think about how much it is going to help me out on Friday nights, it is all worth it in the end.

Another example of this is when It is raining really hard, and it is extremely hard to throw the football. I will end up having to run the ball a lot more, but I still must make sure that I can throw the ball decently. It helps when I have good receivers to bail me out of situations and catch a bad ball. I remind myself to get comfortable with being uncomfortable when I drop back to pass and there is someone coming at me unblocked or the pocket starts to collapse. I have to improvise and start running outside of the pocket while still keeping my eyes downfield to find a receiver and let them go make a play if I throw it to them.

Obviously, that is a really uncomfortable situation, but I just have to think to myself what coach Marshall said against Hartshorne that day.

I am put in a lot of uncomfortable spots, and so does everyone else. This quote relates to me in so many different ways, and I can use it a lot. I am sure that it relates to anyone else that I would ask as well. This is what the meaning of the phrase, "get comfortable with being uncomfortable" means to me.

Gone

By Callie Cooper (Finalist)

The shrill sound of the whistle being blown brings me back down to the game happening around me. I watch as our offense struggles to keep the other team from getting a first down. I sat on the bench, a towel around my neck, leaning over my knees. I listen to the screams of the fans in the stadium, cheering on the team when they tackle the receiver. The fans are excited with how this season has gone so far, you can feel the excitement buzzing through the air. This season is my season, it's my chance to be something more. I'm a senior this year, there are whispers in the air about where i'll be drafted, my coach and my agent both say I'm a shoe in for round one draft picks. I don't care what round I'm drafted in, as long as I am. The whistle rings out again, alerting me that it's time for me to take the field. I line up behind our center, calling out the play.

As I yell hut the center snaps the ball back to me, I begin scanning the field looking for my receivers. I don't see an opening and I have linebackers running at me. I grip the ball and sprint forward. I weave through the defensive line, I'm 30 yards from the endzone, I can feel the wind rushing past my face. I'm 20 yards away when I feel the linebacker running at me from my right. It's almost as if the hit happens in slow motion, I can tell that this is going to hurt before it even happens. The guy drills into my right side, tackling me to the ground.

Searing pain erupts from my left arm. I can't think of anything beyond the prayers that I am sending to the man that has only heard me speak twice in my life. Please I beg within my head, don't let this happen. I can't let this happen. I don't hear the whistle being blown, I can't focus on what the trainer is saying to me. All I can hear is my begging, begging to let my arm be ok.

As I am carried off of the field, I try to focus on anything other than the truth. I zone in on my coach's voice, "How bad is it?"

"Not great, coach" says the team doctor.

"Will he play this season?" The doctor doesn't say anything, "Will he be able to finish this season?" repeated coach

"I do not believe so" stated the doctor.

Ringing began in my ears, I felt warm tears rolling down my face. The voice in my head repeated, "It's all gone... It's all gone... It's all gone" It played on repeat until I drifted into unconsciousness.

Jr. Year

By Emily Gard (Finalist)

From my experience taking an online Latin course, I understood the challenges of learning remotely. I consider myself a hardworking and persistent student, yet the online format still proved difficult to me because there was less contact with the teacher, which led to less dialogue, and made it harder to stay on top of work and process new information. Thus, my first online course, though a beginner's course, taught me how to successfully navigate remote learning.

Then Covid hit. My school system informed us that we would have to be either hybrid or complete remote learning, and my heart sank. I knew from my experience that students could struggle in either system, which is exactly what happened. Not long into the school year, most students, including many of my friends, began to see diminished academic performance, negative psychological effects, and burnout. I knew that I could not accept this, so after I got my bearings, I took charge of the situation to become a leader to those around me. In order to make this work, I had chosen hybrid so I could better meet deadlines, and have an easier time connecting with teachers. Because many students went online instead, I needed to help them in almost every aspect. For example, one of my friends was forced online because he had to work at his parent's restaurant, help his little sister with her schoolwork, and had no car, so I stepped up to offer help. I was more than up for the challenge and was happy to use my academic skills and previous experience to help other students. I went in full force facilitating communication with teachers, transporting and providing materials and resources, conducting online tutoring sessions, and relaying dates and deadlines. As the year went on, I became the go-to person for many of my friends if they needed help with anything academic. Together we created this strong system of support that benefited us all. Last year was far from perfect. However, through my contributions, I helped to make this terrible situation just a little better.

Michael the Archangel

By Samantha Hall (Second Place Winner 2022)

Michael placed his hand on the hilt of his sword as he stood in the grassy field. Lucifer would meet him any second now in this field to battle for his place on the throne of The Kingdom of Heaven. Follow me, and I will create a better kingdom. I will show you a new and better way. He had bribed Michael with the idea of leaving Heaven and creating a new life for themselves. He claimed that he was far superior to God, that his perfection surpassed that of their creator, and thus they should follow him and his ways.

Michael heard the sound of a sword being brought forth from its sheath and was shaken out of his thoughts. Lucifer stood a few yards away from him with a sinister grin on his face. Michael choked back the tears that threatened to spill from his eyes. "Lucifer...I don't want to fight you."

"Well, your drawn sword would suggest otherwise," the Angel scoffed.

"You can't win. Father God is too strong. You can't rebel simply because you think you're better than him."

"Oh, I'm afraid I can. I am the best angel he created. The most magnificent Cherubim Angel that he created to serve him at his throne. I am the most perfect, most beautiful, most powerful angel that our Father has created. I have better ideas to expand this kingdom, far greater ideas. His "all-loving" nature is what's keeping us from expanding."

"Lucifer, Father's knowledge is far superior to yours. He sets an example for how we should love one another. You only love yourself! You're a traitor."

"I'm not a traitor! If anything I'm a savior; freeing my comrades from the one we called 'Father'. I shall become their new leader, their new hero...their new God."

"WHO IS LIKE GOD?"

Michael charged at him and swung his sword at him. Lucifer dodged and tried to strike him, but was blocked and their swords collided. The attacker cried out in rage as Michael ducked and slid between his legs and tried to impale him. Lucifer dodged and lunged at his former friend, holding the sword above his head and prepared to strike. Michael felt the air of the sword swish past him as the blade just barely missed his head.

Lucifer ripped his sword out of the ground. "I tried to make this work. I tried to get you on my side. I always believed that you would stand by me no matter what. And yet, the moment I needed you the most, you abandoned me!"

His sword clashed against Michael's. The archangel gritted

his teeth as he pushed back. "I never abandoned you. I would never leave your side; I loved you Lucifer, and I still do. It was you who abandoned me!"

In the blink of an eye, Michael ducked and rolled out of the way and kicked him in the gut. "You betrayed Father! You betrayed us all!" As the enemy tried to thrust his sword into Michael's ribs, the angel struck the sword and sent it flying from his hand. He knocked Lucifer to the ground and pressed his foot on his head, ready to strike.

Lucifer waited for the strike to come, but it never came. He felt Michael lift his foot from his head. "Get out," the Warrior growled.

The rebel rolled onto his back and looked up at him. "What?"

Michael had a loose grip on his sword and his eyes were downcast. "I said...get out. If you want to leave Father and all of us, fine; But I refuse to fight you."

In a fit of rage, Lucifer leapt to his feet and lunged at him. Michael ducked out of the way, grabbed him by the collar of his armor, and flung him across the field and sent him crashing through The Gates of Heaven. The golden gates closed behind him, leaving Lucifer standing there in wrathful anger.

Michael was sprawled out on his bed as he stared at the golden ceiling; the battle replaying over and over again in his mind. There was a knock and Father God opened the door to the room. "Mind if I join you, My Son?"

Michael sat up on his bed, resting from such a wearisome battle. "No, Father. I don't mind."

He sat on the edge of the bed and placed his hand on his cheek. "You've done a great deed for this Kingdom, Michael. The entirety of Heaven is indebted to you."

The archangel couldn't hold the tears back any longer as his Father pulled him into his arms and cradled his head on his shoulder. "I-I...I miss him, Father. Why did he rebel?" Michael's voice cracked and he pressed his face into God's chest. "Why wouldn't he listen to you?"

"Ssshhh my son. Sssshhh. I miss him too, and I always will. It breaks my heart to know that he wasn't happy here, along with many of my sons and daughters. Lucifer was one of the first Cherubim angels I created. He was considered handsome and powerful by all of you, and I'm afraid that those gifts went to his head. He believed that through his power, he could overthrow me and create a new kingdom. However, Lucifer's mind has been corrupted with Pride, and if he were to rule, this Kingdom and everything outside it would fall into chaos. My son, you did no wrong thing. You have done something great that will be remembered for eternity."

Michael snuggled against His chest. "Father...his pride forced me to fight him. It forced me to kick him out."

"No one forced you to do anything, Michael. I offered to defeat Lucifer myself. But you, child, were willing to stand up to him and represent The Kingdom of Heaven. You chose to fight for this home. And I am so, so proud of you, my son."

One Forty-Nine

By Rowan (Finalist)

If I had left one minute later after my English 11 class, would that have mattered? If my class hadn't persuaded the sub to let us leave just one minute earlier, would that have saved me from losing function in my brain for six months? Leaving the classroom at 1:49 PM felt like a field day just one minute before the bell. Giggling down the hallway on my way to the parking lot, my classmates and I were in a rush to get to our cars because being the last person to arrive meant being stuck in the swelling traffic of the parking lot. For once I could get to my spot on time and beat the traffic.

As the bell rang for classes to end and witnessing the students rushing out of their classes, I speed-walked even faster. As I stepped out the front door and started running towards my white Honda Accord, I saw my four-door car with a Bengals sticker on the back on the bumper looking right at me. As I unlocked my car, I threw my door open and dropped my backpack off the side of my right shoulder; my 1,000-pound book bag decided to take me down with it. With my hands full of books and my leftover lunch, my head became the hands that should have broken my fall. Everything went black and quiet. I couldn't hear the students chattering around me. Eventually, when I regained my thoughts, I threw my still dangling book bag into the back seat and sat in front of the wheel. I shut my door and started to feel the ache in my neck and stabbing pain in the right side of my forehead. I thought to myself, "What would one minute have done?"

Soon after, I was stuck in the doctor's office listening to them explain how there were three grades of a concussion. Grade one is mild and lasts less than 15 minutes and involves no loss of consciousness. Grade two is moderate with symptoms that last longer than 15 minutes and involve no loss of consciousness. Grade three is losing consciousness and healing very slowly and with a high risk of permanent brain damage. When I heard my diagnosis was grade three I felt numb. I couldn't comprehend what he was saying. I was lucky to not suffer permanent brain damage. However, I did end up having speech difficulties due to damage to the left hemisphere. I also had damage to my cerebellum which made me lose my balance and affected my coordination. The right temporal lobe was a big effect on processing my sensory information and difficulties of also understanding spoken words and retaining new information which made school very challenging.

I didn't realize how much we rely on our bodies until I couldn't balance and walk in a straight line. Damaging the most important part of your body contributes to slowness and an inability to perform functions. When I had my concussion, I couldn't cheer for six months. I had to go to therapy for four months to help me heal.

We have 206 bones in our body and 600 muscles—thinking about how the body functions 24 hours a day is amazing. Walking and running is a blessing because I know my concussion has had so much effect on learning and processing information that it was a challenge. If everyone including myself would have more patience it could actually protect us from the unexpected and possibly a bad outcome. Have patience because even if it is just for one minute that one minute can change everything.

Rare

By Aurora Rutkowski (Finalist)

Liver function, Biopsy, Ultrasound, Treatment Plan. Four years ago these concepts would have been unknown to me. Each an experience out of my reach. Now, I find they infest my daily routine, pushing aside my life for their priority.

Rare is just another term for unique, but what's so unique about a chronic disease that changes your life? Being diagnosed with a serious illness at a young age is hard; but what about when that illness rarely affects your age group, its cause is unknown, and nobody understands your struggles. I would be lying if I said I never found myself asking, "why me?". Considering people usually say it's because I'm "strong", maybe it's a simple question.

The lessons I learned didn't come that easy. The process

was straining mentally and physically, it became hard to see the strength everyone kept referencing.

My summer physical turned into 24 hours of waiting for ultrasound results. My diagnosis process was over the course of a few weeks. At this point, a week had never felt so prolonged, especially when being surrounded by sterile hospital walls that seemed to enclose me as my eyes traced the room out of boredom. Laying on crunchy bed paper was an experience tormenting to hear as I tried to get comfortable waiting for various doctors, passing through my room like I was a new exhibit still being researched. My summer vacation was a tour around the children's hospital, making stops at a new floor each time a test came back negative. As I leveled up from one doctor to another, my prize was another hospital band and a different colored blood vial.

When diagnosed, the one aspect of your disease they fail to mention is the way it changes your life. As time passed after my initial diagnosis, not only did my body change but my view changed. The beginning of my health journey was harder than imaginable. I can recall kids making fun of me for my rounder appearance. What they didn't realize was that the medication saving my life was the cause of my weight gain. How do you explain this concept to kids in your grade?

I couldn't; I suffered in silence.

Simultaneously, my health battle was ongoing given I struggled with other health concerns outside of my rare disease. I wanted to be done with the name-calling, the tests, and consultations. It felt as though I couldn't catch a break. I lost hope.

Reflecting back from where I am today, I learned that you can lift yourself up in a time of adversity and face your challenge head on, if you change your mindset and your perspective.

When I feel disparagingly, I remind myself that one adversity is not an end-all, tomorrow is a new opportunity.

As my perspective changed, consequently my morals changed. Given my own experience, I try to view the world through acknowledgement of other people; always keeping in mind that others are facing their own battles. My definition of sympathy and empathy changed. I always try to project the kindness I wish I had onto others because, whatever one's challenge may be, kindness may not fix the issue but it creates a foundation of support when others need it most. In respect to my own personal growth, I learned self advocacy and responsibility. Not only do I have to hold myself accountable when it comes to upkeep of my health, but I also find myself claiming responsibility when it comes to academics and leadership.

Self advocacy is a value I have been working towards over the past four years. Self regulation and awareness is a strength I've come to follow. In hard situations such as athletics, the classroom, and my personal life I have built the courage to speak for not only myself but also others in need.

The Creature Inside Me

By Nicholas D. Hagedorn (Finalist)

In sixth grade, I wanted to be Vincent van Gogh. Not for his painting skills, but because I too wanted to cut off my left ear — both ears, actually. Cutting them off would be less painful than every second they stayed on. Who needs hearing, anyway? Sign language seemed sufficient.

But day after day this solution seemed more infeasible. The vile creature inside of me festered, spread. It started to explore its habitat, venturing outside my ear. It slithered down my throat, wrapped its tentacles around my skin, and squeezed. Hard. It put up a defensive shield around my body: Anything that breathed on my skin turned into a swarm of mosquitoes, draining my energy and not the creature's. In our parasitic relationship, the creature neither lived off my flesh nor my blood. It lived off my pain.

The creature's name evolved throughout the years. It was first labeled acute otitis media when I was in 4th grade, though I dubbed it "Ear Infection." Catchy, I know. My family did the natural thing: We went to my pediatrician. I had known him — or rather he had known me — since I was born. When I was younger, I would always surprise him when he asked what my favorite food was.

"Broccoli," I would respond, though sometimes I said "Asparagus."

I felt comfortable around him. I knew that he would always be able to help me.

"I'm going to look to see if there are any monkeys in your ears."

He shines his flashlight into my right ear, followed by my left ear.

"Nick does have an ear infection," he tells my mother.

It seems nothing out of the ordinary; I had suffered from a wave of ear infections when I was two years old. In fact, he is the same pediatrician who helped me through those earlier troubles. Though this new infection is painful, it is completely manageable. I don't wail and scream like I did when I was two. But this particular ear infection poses another challenge that makes it distinct: It won't go away.

"That's odd," my pediatrician comments during our follow-up appointment.

He looks inside my ear once again.

"The infection looks like it's all cleared up. Are you sure still feel the pai—"

"Yes," I respond.

"I'll have to refer you to an ear specialist. They are called ENT doctors. 'ENT' stands for 'Ear Nose & Throat.'"

We walk out of the clinic. He doesn't say it explicitly, but I realize my pediatrician doesn't know what is wrong with me.

"Mom, does he not know what is in my ear?"

"No one knows everything, Nick."

That may be true — and it may be obvious — but I'd never had to confront this fact before. Every day I went to school and learned mathematics, English, history, and science. My teachers taught because they knew what they were teaching. Sure, my elementary school mathematics teacher likely didn't know calculus, but he knew what was needed to properly teach and answer all the class's questions.

A few months later, we visit the ENT doctor. He refers us to a different kind of specialist. A few months later, we visit another doctor, who refers us to yet another. Every doctor looks at me, mutters to himself, and checks some records before coming up with a new name for the creature inside me. Some doctors have their own cures — surgery, or medicine which may not be the most scientific — and some doctors are just confused. None of the doctors' cures ever work.

My family becomes desperate for answers. When you're desperate for answers, you find clues where none exist. And we were desperate. My dad would spend hours every night looking through every medical page on the internet to try to find something, anything related to what was wrong with me.

We think I might have a dairy allergy, so I stop eating dairy. We think there might be a pressure issue on the eardrum, so I start obsessively chewing gum. And so on, every fix a bit more far-fetched than the last. Each might have helped briefly — I'm not sure — but the pain continues to persist. These changes are significant because they are small. Removing dairy from my diet was just one of numerous ways my life was forced to change from fear of the creature inside me. Each change by itself is manageable, translucent. To an outsider, my life appears the same after a new treatment is painted onto my routine. Yet one modification follows another, and another, and another. With every coat of paint, my true self sinks deeper beneath the increasingly opaque layers of attempted cures. I drift farther from whom I used to be.

Eventually, we will learn that I have Amplified Musculoskeletal Pain Syndrome, a chronic pain disorder caused by a pain-feedback loop in my nervous system, transforming small events like a breeze in the wind into the pain of being stabbed with a knife. We will learn that Amplified Musculoskeletal Pain Syndrome doesn't have a cure; "for these teens, the only way to overcome pain is to face it," reads a recent WHYY article on Amplified Musculoskeletal Pain Syndrome. The creature will gradually, slowly, vanish from my body. Even then, a small part of it will always stay with me. But for now, I don't know what I have. For now, WHYY hasn't published their article on Amplified Musculoskeletal Pain Syndrome; chronic pain in children has not yet become as well-known as it is in 2022. So for now, my sixth-grade self and my family are desperate. And I will never forget that feeling of desperation, no matter how small my creature—my Amplified Musculoskeletal Pain Syndrome—gets.

The Importance of a Speck of Dust

By Rebecca Lorenz (First Place Winner 2022)

I always loved clouds as a child

Wisps of white in the blue sky

Forming what we were silly to think of as faces

Until I got my own cloud

But this cloud, unlike the childlike wonder and joy of the old ones

Is dark, and tired

And it follows me everywhere

It began in the back of my mind with daily thoughts and fears of not being enough

But slowly, as I got older, it began to consume my whole being

It was all I thought about

Wondering how even in a group full of people I felt so alone

With the people who used to bring me so much joy all I could think of was going home

And nothing ever seemed to fully fill that emptiness.

Like a sled barreling down a dark hill, gaining traction and speed with every second

Going faster and faster, taking slowly your ability to steer

Until you're completely out of control, going full speed down the hill

Like going 60 on a residential street at 12am with no headlights on

Until it's-

November 15th, 2019

I'm sitting in the bathroom, my whole body shaking as my mouth tastes the liquid salt that is my tears

That salt being the closest thing I've had to food in the past 29 hours

My eyes not breaking contact with the bottle of extra strength tylenol on the counter

The tension of a solution in front of my face is like heroin in front of an addict

It was a concert but the band wasn't there, only the throbbing and high pitched feedback of the speakers in my head

I couldn't do it anymore

Why was everything so-

Loud.

I had made my peace

I mean sure, people would be sad

Some for a week, some for a month, maybe even a year

But at the end of the day, the world still spins

And life moves on because it has to

And I am but one octillionth a part of our solar system

And in that moment that was exactly how I felt.

Like a speck of dust

An insignificant obscurity in the darkness of the universe

All my friends ever heard from their parents was to be more like me

And they were as sick of it as I was

Because who was I?

I have no idea of who I really am.

All I've ever wanted was to be liked

I would change the way I talked or dressed or stood

Simply because the thought of being alone and hated by everyone scared me more than not recognizing the girl in the mirror

I grew up petrified that someday the people around me were going to hate me as much as I hated myself

I grew up afraid of the monsters in the dark that slowly morphed into the monsters in my brain

Those same monsters that pushed me to the edge

The edge of November 15th in the bathroom

Looking off of that edge, I thought of my parents

Of course they noticed the skipping classes,

But not the skipping meals

I hated the idea of a girl who wasn't even real

They noticed the dropping grades

But not the dropping weight

Just go ahead, swallow them, all of them, no need to wait

But wait

My parents will think that they could have done better

And those what-if thoughts will eat into their hearts forever

I spent so long advocating that everyone's feelings are valid

And I poured those feelings into all of my ballads

So why can't anyone fix me?

Looking at the bottle I think

This is the only way that I can ever be truly free

But I owe it to myself to try for a future, even if I can't see

So I finally break the tension of my gaze to the bottle

Take a deep breath

And walk into my Mom's room

I had avoided this for so long

I didn't want to tell my Mom that I didn't want to live

In the body that she created with her own being

Her little girl she spent 9 months crafting herself

But that talk

That vulnerability

Is what saved my life.

Now I'm here and I can see my future for the first time in what seems like forever

The future that my past self tried to imagine, but her brain wouldn't let her

I'm going to college

And I'm taking advantage of every moment

I'm building my future with myself as the main component

And taking mental notes of everything I would have missed since that day.

So here's my list as follows from then to today;

I would have missed eating pesto cavatappi one last time

Finding a lot of non-corny ways to rhyme

I would have missed getting into college

Finally getting my hard work acknowledged

Oh and also I would have missed turning 18

And finding the boy straight out of my 7 year old dreams

I would have missed the warm feeling of the sun on my face

And using my privilege to advocate for the equality of race

Playing my songs every Sunday night in the summer

Getting cut off by a car with a live laugh love sticker on the bumper

So yes, this is my list and hopefully it keeps growing

Not all the days are great but I finally have the will to keep going

I keep going to relate to anyone who's in a similar place

It's not weakness and you're not burden to ask anyone for help

Because it's the worst type of loneliness to try to do it by yourself.

The Storm

By Rebecca Gardner (Finalist)

Everything was quiet except the wind whispering worries throughout the deserted neighborhood. In a small backyard I stood underneath an old swing set pushing the swing back and forth. My little cousin's hair whipped with the wind as the swing creaked with each push. The gray sky loomed above us, silently screaming as if it were about to start roaring in frustration. Still the swing went back and forth. From inside the yellow house the news report could be heard, "...the winds are up to 180 miles per hour." The voice droned on and the lights that flooded in the yard flickered on and off. Still the swing went back and forth. I slowly lifted my head up at the dull, cloudy sky at the same moment a bright light flashed above, creating angry tentacles that raced through the atmosphere. The light in the house burned out and the reporter's voice abruptly stop. We jumped at the new phenomenon and recoiled into the house. Still the swing set went back and forth, this time with the violent, reckless wind. The thunder boomed loudly, shaking the house as I heard a piercing scream.

Instantly my hand went to cover my mouth and the screaming stopped. The rain started drowning out everything as it hit the roof in large drops. I sat down in a lopsided circle, my family surrounding me as a candle flickered to light, casting shadows all around the room. As we wait for what tomorrow brings, we got out a board game, The Game of Life. Starting up the game everyone almost forgot about the raging storm outside. But then the house vibrates and shakes with the powerful storm as the thunder cried out and lightning streaked across the sky. "It's your turn honey," my mother calmly claimed in a soothing voice. She was trying to distract us from the terrifying thought of what was going to come next, so on we played. The clock hand reached a late hour, and it was decided that we all go to sleep, or try to. Walking our separate ways, I stood in my doorway. I took stiff steps until I reached the comfort of my soft bed. While I laid on the mattress, I stared at the white ceiling above me, shadows dancing across it. The wind outside howled like a wolf on a full moon. The wind tore threw the trees and a soft murmur could be heard just below my window. I cautiously sprung out of bed and creeped over to the window, keeping my head low. Again the murmur continued this time sounding more agitated than before. I peaked my head over the glass, my head heavy from lack of sleep and whirling with worries of what was to come. An axe murderer? Kidnapper? Lost child stuck in the storm? A bird flapping it wings and fighting again the ferocious downpour? My eyes level with the crystal clear glass, and I squint to see into the darkness. I jump as an unexpected murmur sounded against the glass, more tremendous than ever before. Shivering in anticipation I peek again as the murmur starts.

My body relaxes as I see a branch pulled back from the wind, whipping around creating the horrible sound. I climb back into the comfort of my bed. While the storm rages on around me, I fall into an uneasy sleep. All around me destruction occurs—flying objects, flooded houses, power outages, and yet I still doze off, cowering in my corner. Suddenly my eyes peel open, and I see light flooding in my room. Even though the natural light brightens my room, I stand up and try the light switch. Up and down, up and down. There was no soft glow of the bulb or any speeding of the fan from above. I went out in the hallway to check the light switch there. Up and down, up and down. Still no response. As I walked around the house I noticed it slowly getting hotter, as there was no flow of air anywhere in the abode. Once I had wandered through every crook and cranny I gazed out of the window, even though the sky was covered in dark, restless gray clouds, you could see the light shining through. Outside there was no breeze blowing in the air nor rain dropping from the sky. On the floor, tree limbs were scattered everywhere, dead grass spread out everywhere.

However, a pink splatter of color sat in the middle of the yard among all the gray. Curiously I made my way over to it. There in the middle of the yard one beautiful pink flower bloomed in all of this misery. After seeing that one beautiful flower, I thought it was a sign, maybe the storm was over, maybe it would never happen again? Soon I would experience another, but in the meantime all I could think about was that flower. How could something so pure want to bloom after so much havoc was brought upon it?

Words on a Screen

By Ara Colby (Finalist and Honorable Mention)

"I'm on my way."

I press send with my right hand; the other on the wheel. I bring my gaze back to the windshield when I realize I've made the worst mistake of my life. My car collides with the one in front of me and the force of the impact throws my body forward. Glass shatters and tires screech against the asphalt. My head hurts. Thick liquid drips into my eyes. The awareness of my decision hurts more than anything else. Did I just unknowingly decide that a text message was worth more than a human life?

.....

I brake at the red light and crane my neck to meet the eyes of my two crazy children.

"Miranda and Noah. For God's sake, please calm down just a little bit. I love your singing, but Mommy's trying to drive." My little Noah grimaces and Miranda smiles with dimples that could brighten the sun. I smile back at my two angels.

"Okay, Mommy." Miranda answers. "I love you, Mommy." She adds. My heart warms at those words.

"I love-" all of a sudden, my body is thrown onto the steering wheel and my forehead crashes onto the dashboard. Before I can gather what happened, my car is pushed further into the intersection and we're spinning. All I can think of is how I didn't get to tell them how much I love them.

.....

"Olivia! How could you say that?" I say with mock horror. She's giggling like crazy. A smile plays on my lips.

"Well it's true, isn't it?" She squeaks. She's still laughing hysterically.

"Whatever." I say with an eye roll. "Now calm down and hold my hand" The crosswalk sign blinks with an icon of a walking man. Olivia groans.

"Stop being a big sister. I'm old enough to walk by myself!"

"Nope." I state. I grasp her hand and begin to cross with her at my side. She struggles, but soon realizes I won't relent.

We're almost to the sidewalk when she cries, "Wait!"

Her fingers wiggle out of my tight grasp and she runs back into the middle of the road. Then she bends over to grab something.

"Olivia!" I scream, "The light is about to-" I don't get to

finish my sentence when I see my worst fear unfold before my eyes. About ten feet away, where my sister is crouched on the crosswalk, I see a car speed into the one in front of it. The car taking the impact flies forward to where my oblivious sister holds a penny in her hand. Then she's gone. I can't move. The car that took my life and soul away from me, is now in the middle of the intersection. It gets hit by a second car coming from another direction; sending it spinning. My knees buckle and I fall to the ground. I don't even care that I'm in the middle of the road. I just need to go back to the moment where my little sister's warm hand was safely in mine.

.....

The TV's volume is up all the way. There are sirens in the background as the news reporter speaks, "There were four deaths today as the result of a major car accident. The woman who caused the crash died from internal bleeding just after she was brought to the hospital. Two children were in the car she hit and the police say they died instantly. Another little girl's life was taken while she crossed the road with her sister. He pauses, "How many deaths will it take for you to learn?" He pauses again, staring into the camera with sad eyes. The eyes of someone who's both witnessed and felt heartbreaking loss. He sighs, "Don't text and drive. This is Jared, see you tomorrow at CNN."

Work over Will?

By Morgan Smith (Finalist)

Heart beats fast. Suffocating pounds, tingling toes and fingers. I leap from the dusty ground, calves kissing hamstrings jolting the muscles awake. The heat of anticipation closes in, the tips of shoes digging deep into the starting line. Last minute shoe tying, hair tying, shirt tying, and gulps of fear are silenced by daunting steps. No sound is made, only listening ears to the man in red. He grips the cool metal standing aside, raising his arms. The ear piercing boom of the gun rings through the crowd, shuffling feet and heavy breaths leave behind the fleeting anxiety transformed into burning adrenaline.

Hope can't save me now, only strength, endurance, delusion. Breathing is consistent, insync with pumping arms and screaming legs. Power and pain driving each bound, each twist and turn of the path laughing at the tired expressions. I pass the whimpers, and blank moments with the crumble of cracking mud my only comfort. The echo of voices erupts from the road ahead, shouts of wonder and passion drowned out by the clinging and clanging of a cow bell.

Once again, a calming quiet, clearing the mind from stress and agony, just put one foot in front of the other. It gets easier, as you feel stronger but the sweat stings my eyes, glistening in the fading sun.

Time ticks differently here, dragging on but counting down quicker than ever. Running a race against the clock. I'm sure it's near the end now, the few victims surrounding letting out exhausted breaths. I sprint and fall back into place swerving between ones who have given up, ones who just can't go any more. I feel the adrenaline wavering as I drift across the slippery slope. The mountain rises higher as I climb, dust slithering up my legs, clumping with drowning sweat trickling down my neck, coating my skin in a ghastly color. The top is almost serene, a cool October breeze mixed with the drizzle of a coming rain. Clouds drifting and watching in amusement. But this is not something I have time to notice as I fall back to level ground. The trek continues but the steps become harder. Splats of mud cake my shoes and peaceful sprinkles soak braided hair. The spray of the rain tickles my eyelashes forcing clammy fingers to wipe the anguish away. Sky darkens with an angering pour and the loss of people surrounding. Only a few remain.

She falls in line beside me, the panting, the groveling, the pumping, and the groaning. Our pace doesn't falter, our fates are intertwined now. She inches ahead, I reach forward with desire. I move to the inside and she claws her way to my shoulder. The clock ticks on as do the cheers, the ringing, and clomping of feet. Each slush of my foot races with competition, passion pushing past pain.

Let the mind games begin—

We know that we are evenly paced, one in the same, both wanting to win, both worked hard, both strong and cutthroat, willing to do whatever it takes. It's only a matter of time before I pass her, we think. She is tired too. Watch the stride, listen to the breathing, let her go and save your energy. The smallest battles are won in simple strategy and ego boosting. If I slow down she moves forward but the adrenaline only lasts for a moment and that is when you strike. Let her come next to you, let her push and push but once she starts to sync with your stride, you sprint. Cause the willingness to be faster to waver with each knock down. Make her believe that you still have the energy to kick when she does not.

The course lets out into a strip to the finish. The endurance won't help you here, here it is speed, the switching of the form, back straightened, arms tightened. Knees reach higher with all that I have left. Leaping figures filled with color and noise decorate the pathway, screams drive the last bits of anything. Who truly wants it more?

She desperately scrambles to the side poking into my peripheral vision. But I am stronger, I have the kick but just not yet. She seems to enjoy the moment of triumph but that is all it really is. For she did not wait for the perfect time to invade. She realizes her mistake as I pull forward with confidence and torture. The purple mats beep in the joyous sound of ending, the tracking of the time, milliseconds ahead, but ahead nonetheless. Deathly drops of victory fall down my face, dirt stained skin and sinister smiles of relief, the cool body of the medal sends chills coursing down my spine with each embrace of sticky and rain soaked teammates. Breathy good jobs and cries of excitement and disappointment fill the air.

Races can't be won by luck or pure motivation, manifestation, or teamwork. It's all based on what you are truly capable of. What have you trained for, built endurance for, stretched and single handedly strived for? They can be predicted and preserved, you are only as good as the miles on your feet.

The refreshing, earthy smell and taste of the dripping storm cool my body to its core. The heat is gone and I begin to shiver.

SECTION 3 – LOVE

Diary of a Raincloud

By Chase Pickford (Finalist)

POV: Nimbus

I've always dreamt of being a Cumulus cloud. Who wouldn't want to be the cotton candy of the sky, to be full and complete. To be admired, able to elegantly glide over the world with the wind beneath my vapor. Even the word Cumulus incites joy, originating from the word cumulo, meaning heap or pile of clouds. A Cumulus, by definition, is never without company. Whereas, Nimbus literally translates to a large gray rain cloud. It's insulting, truly, to be named after an uncontrollable emotional state. After all, no one would name their child "freaks out in public" or "screams when frustrated." Despite what some rays of sunshine might tell me, I really am defined by my actions.

It's not that I want to be sad, no one wants to be sad. I just can't help it. Take today, for instance, today is a beautiful day. Unfortunately, I happen to hate beautiful days. The sun is shining, the flowers are blooming, it's almost as if the whole world is smiling. But when the whole world is smiling, it really makes me wonder why I can't. I might try it for a moment, being happy, but it just doesn't feel right. Happiness should be a feeling, not a role to be played. So why is it so easy for others to be happy but so hard for me? Beautiful days only emphasize that I do not belong. That I will never belong. After all, I have no part to play on a beautiful day, all the roles are already filled. To participate is to rain on someone else's parade, literally. But sometimes I can't help myself.

Today is one of those times. The whole world seems to mock me with its brightness. It would be so easy to let myself drift and expand through the sky, stretching my arms. To cast a long glum shadow on the land below and stare at my undefined shape. To blindfold the sun with my body, causing the world to reflect the foggy uncertainty I feel. But I can't. I know if I start, I won't be able to stop. It's a slippery slope between a shower and a hurricane, and I'd rather not discover that slope. I just can't. I repeat this to myself, hoping it will convince me, but it is only met with discouraging whispers from the wind. "I can't," I say, ever be normal it seems to whisper, unwelcomingly completing my thoughts. "I can't" I repeat louder, do anything right it counters. "I can't," be happy. "I can't," be likeable. "I can't-I can't-I can't" I scream until my voice turns raspy.

Be good enough, it finishes.

There is a halting silence for a moment. The birds scatter. They know as well as I do, this is the calm before the storm. The wind forms an anthem that fills my soul, chanting my downfalls, whispering my insecurities, and finally speaking the truth. "I can't" I say, knowing it's already too late. I am already forming raindrops, becoming heavy with the sadness I've carried for too long. The sponge that is my heart has been squeezed, and I can no longer prevent the sadness from oozing away.

My world goes dark and I begin to hear the rhythmic pitter-patter of my baneful existence.

POV: Mr. Jensen

"Grab a jacket!" my daughter yells worriedly. But I am already fumbling to slide my yellow rain boots on, never mind finding a jacket. As my wife used to say, "Rain waits for no one."

I walk as fast as I can manage down the steps of my house, barely noticing as the door slams behind me. I take a deep breath in and hold it for a moment, tasting the air as it floods my system. I let its freshness settle in my chest for a moment. Everything that seemed to matter only seconds ago is washed away. Jacketless, the rain hits my bare skin and runs down my face. I laugh, feeling silly that something as simple as rain can still bring me so much joy, even at the age of seventy-eight. But how could it not? All the best things in my life happened when it rained. It's becoming harder and harder to remember those things. Dr. Nelson says eventually I won't remember them at all. But the rain seems to make everything clear. I can almost see it when I close my eyes, I can almost see her.

The streets become glossy with moisture. Vibrant reflections of shop signs skip over the newly glossed surface, creating a brilliant kaleidoscope on the once dull asphalt. A young woman dances in the street, her eyes shining with wonder. She leaps through the air with only gravity to hold her from taking flight. With each landing, a small splash erupts, joining the larger orchestra. She is oblivious to the people around her, to the cars passing by, to the blinking lights. To her, there is only the rain, and it is her symphony.

I open my eyes and let my tears mix with the rain. "Thank you..." I whisper to the sky, "for the memories."

POV: Nimbus

He's so quiet, I almost don't hear him. But his words flood into his tears, combining with my own. I see it now, the streets, the lights, the young lovers. They dance in my sadness, illuminating the space around them with a simple glance. To him, my tears are not a sign of weakness. They are not the pitfalls of what I can't be. They are the symbols of what I can. He lets my tears wash his troubles away and rejoices in my rhythmic song. To him, I have recreated the most beautiful day of all: the day he met the love of his life.

I feel my heart swell once more, but this time it's a different kind of weight.

I dare call them tears of joy.

Fated (Not) to Last

By Erika Prophete (Finalist)

"Again!"

Akira snarled, lifting the shinai and forcefully slashing it in a downward arc. It was hot outside, too hot. Definitely too hot to be doing the same drill over and over again. Especially when Chisuke was just standing there, arms crossed like she was better than him or something.

All it took was a blink.

Akira stared up at the sky blankly, letting out an exhale of air as a foot landed on his chest. Chisuke glared down at him blankly, dark bangs moved out of the way and exposing equally dark blue eyes. "I am better than you, stupid! And learn how to keep the few thoughts you do have in that thick skull of yours!" Each word was punctuated with a harsh poke to his forehead.

She picked up his fallen shinai, slinging it over her shoulder and stepping back. Her chin was lifted, expression haughty and smug. "Be glad I'm helping you get stronger.

Someone has to keep me entertained around here."

He ignored her, sitting up to brush at his white shirt petulantly. His teeth were bared, part of it being resentment-- at his own weakness-- and another part angry at getting caught off guard so easily. Akira put out his hand, cracking a smile when Chisuke clasped it and pulled him up. Like always, he silently marveled at her grip strength, fingers long, smooth, and deceptively delicate looking. Chisuke didn't like her hands, but Akira did. Swordsmen didn't have to look strong, they just had to be strong.

And his long time rival had that in spades. He smiled sharply, tightening his hold.

"Let's go again, I'll kick your ass for sure one day."

The girl cackled, an evil little sound as her eyes glinted mischievously. "Look at you, learning so fast like that. Now you're saying 'one day' instead of 'this time' . All I have to do is keep kicking your ass and you'll... be saying... 'never' in... no time."

Chisuke tossed her head back, clutching her stomach with one hand as she broke into a fit of giggles, slowly growing into a loud laugh.

Akira averted his eyes, bottom lip sticking out in what most definitely was not a pout. He unclasped their palms, ignoring the way a part of him protested. It was becoming a familiar feeling, like there was a string tying him to her. Like she was a plug of some sort, and taking her away meant draining Akira.

Instinct told him it'd be a weakness but feelings said

that it was pleasant. Feelings told him that her hair must be soft and the pads of her fingers rough. It urged him to make Chisuke laugh more and poke her cheek where that one dimple was. Feelings were complicated. They made his gaze stray back to where she stood, despite him not wanting to. They made a silly smile grace his young features.

And Chisuke, of course, noticed his staring.

"What're you looking at?" she asked amicably, head cocked to the side.

He gave a short shrug, not sure how to put all the thoughts-- yes he had more than a few -- into words. "You're eyes, they have stars in them."

It was only after they came out that he wondered if what he said made a lick of sense and wasn't just some kind of gibberish.

But she understood, like she always did, if the soft smile directed at him was any indicator. It was the smile that made his heart pound like he was in a fight. Chisuke ruffled his hair affectionately.

"Yeah I get what you mean." she whispered. "You have them too."

Soulmates were a rare thing. Not everyone had them and in fact, it was so rare that poeple feared having one. A soulmate was more than an other half, it was a bond that tied two souls together irrevocably. A bond so strong that if broken, it could drive all parties to insanity. There was little privacy with a soulmate, and the stronger the bond the deeper the connection.

He'd heard about it once, in passing. Soulmates.

A spinner had made their way to his small village, doing as all storytellers did and weaving tales of bonds and strength.

Akira wondered if sharing a goal was the same as sharing a dream, making a promise. He wondered if soulmates made the world brighter--even if it was night and they were crying, tears shining-- and did weird things to his stomach like make it flip flop. He wondered if soulmates could be rivals. He wondered if it could best friends.

His questions never got answered, and it didn't really matter anyways.

Chisuke was dead the next day.

Goodbyes

By Sofia Prieto Black (Finalist)

The heat weighed heavy on my shoulders, beads of sweat rolled down my forehead. I stared at the asphalt beneath my feet, at the loose pieces of gravel, at tiny shards of glass, and closely observed a crushed coke bottle cap that appeared as though it was 20 years old due to the layer of dust that coated it. As they passed, car engines roared and then quickly faded into the distance. The blurry sight of the stoplight, switching from red, then to green, and yellow, distracted me from the pain I felt, but nothing could dissolve the knot in my throat. It had been three hours since I had gotten out of the car. Three hours since I watched them disappear into the horizon. Three hours since I last said goodbye.

'Eduardo, I don't know how else to say this but we're leaving. I haven't told the girls yet, but the move will be in December. Joris got a job in the States, in California. I've been looking for a while now and just recently came upon Piedmont. It's a small town in Oakland. It seems safe and friendly and the girls will get a much better education there. It'll be hard of course, but they'll be happy.' I stared blankly, not quite understanding what I had just heard. It had been six years since the divorce but I had never imagined she would take life itself from me.

I never was accustomed to crying, though tonight, tonight was different. The evening felt to drag on forever, but I was grateful for the time we still had left. I hoped there was a way, something in my power, that could enable me to slow time, to prevent this from ever having to happen. But tonight, I felt anguish. My stomach turned in ways I could never deem possible. I sat on my balcony, watched clouds appear and disappear, counted stars forming constellations, and listened to the sounds of the city: dogs barking in the distance, ocean waves crashing, wind swaying the tall palms. I sat here, from sunset to sunrise. Tonight, I was dying.

I turned the key and sat still in my car. A few minutes had passed until I heard calls from inside the house. I got out and the girls came running down the bright grass. We stood in the street, holding one another. They both squeezed me tightly and cried. It was then I decided to be strong, strong for them. I knelt and gave each of them a kiss on the cheek. Silence surrounded us; no words could describe how we each felt. I looked up and saw her standing at her bedroom window. She watched as they pleaded, '¿por qué Papi, por qué nos tenemos que ir?' I held each of their hands in mine, as I watched tears roll down her cheeks too.

Two weeks passed in which I cried from day to night. Everything around my house, around town, reminded me of them. I pinched myself constantly to wake from this nightmare;

I felt completely alone in the world. Each day, I drove past their school, their house, and sat for hours on the beach. This routine only made the pain grow, I knew nothing would ever be the same.

Sundays were by far the most difficult. These were the days we spent together: pacing up and down the beach's shores, the grocery store's isles, the movie theatre rows. The simplest activities made them happy, made me happy. When three o'clock hit, I felt instant remorse, I would no longer be hearing the school bell ring, watching as they ran out from the white building. No longer would I be able to hold their hands as we walked to the car. Never would we blast the soundtrack of what seemed like hundreds of musicals. Laughter would never fill the car's small interior again.

I stood in the artificially cool air-conditioned pickup hall of the airport. In hand, I held a bouquet of sunflowers, Sofia's favorite, and a box of Ferrero Rocher chocolates for Vale. I had been there for an hour already, waiting impatiently for it to be time. The doors opened and shut as visitors rushed to their families and waved to their friends. I waited, and waited, and waited. Until finally, two small figures, each holding a small carry-on luggage, looked around nervously. I could tell they were just as anxious as I was. Then, we locked eyes. I watched one of the gestures to the other. They both ran, dragging their bags, too heavy for their small arms, beside them. I heard the word I most missed, 'Papi'.

Hiding from the Sun

By Alexandra Marie Chilson (Finalist)

"So, Mr. Lawson, you have the credentials and recommendations we are looking for at our establishment. We would love for you to join us, let's say, Monday at 7:00?"

I smiled and shook his hand and that's when I saw it. A mustard stain. A yellow mustard stain. My smile faded as I stumbled to find words, my heart racing faster by the second. "Um, I, Mr. Steiner you have a little something on your shirt."

He put his hand to his shirt, looked down and laughed "Oh, so I do. I'm sorry I just had lunch. I guess some got on me."

I nodded fast and grabbed a napkin from my pocket, fumbling as I went to grab it. "I-I can help you Mr. Steiner."

He looked at me with an odd look as I reached over to rub out the stain. "No Mr. Lawson, I think I am fully capable. Thank you very much."

I ignored him though as I reached over the desk desperately trying to get the stain. "Mr. Lawson you need to back away now."

I almost reached him when he pushed a button on the phone. "Security to my office now. Please, escort Mr. Lawson out of the building."

My mouth gaped and I backed up, trying to pay attention to the man in front of me while my eyes unintentionally looked down to the stain a couple times. "B-But Mr. Stainer, I mean Steiner, you said I was a perfect candidate! You said Monday at 7:00 to be here for work."

Mr. Steiner rubbed his head in exhaustion. "Yes, Mr. Lawson but now you can wait for our call. We have many other candidates to consider."

I looked between Mr. Steiner, the door and the stain thinking of what to do next. I looked at the stain one more time as I heard the door open and leapt at Mr. Steiner's shirt.

"Everything happened so fast. He said I was the perfect candidate and everything John."

I looked at my friend, John Wilson, who was now driving us back to our apartment as I answered his questions. "Henrick, how did It really go? You were being escorted by security when I pulled up. What happened?"

I looked down at my feet for a second before I decided to answer. "Well, I mean, it's a lot more complicated than you think. He-He had a-a stain on his shirt from his lunch. It was the color and I don't do well with that."

John laughed for a second, then responded, "Yes, I do realize that. I believe I found that out the hard way also."

I looked up at him quickly to see his faint smile on his face. Him finding out about my Xanthophobia the hard way is an understatement. Xanthophobia is the fear of yellow. It is definitely something hard to live with. I mean, I love my life and everything, but I just can't get over this fear. I tried to see someone about it, I really did. I started seeing a psychologist. We started diagnosing my condition and what medication to take and he said it shouldn't take long at all to diagnose me. I have amazing friends and supportive family. I honestly couldn't ask for more, well I mean, I couldn't ask for more, but I will. It gets lonely. All my family and friends have somebody and I'm just, alone. I mean I would love to meet someone who doesn't care about my condition. "Hey, Henry, did you hear me?"

I snapped back to reality and nodded responded quickly. "Yeah, Yeah, of course I did!"

I looked back down as the car slowed down a bit. It must be a yellow light. I heard a chuckle coming from the front seat "So, you're okay with our plan?"

Nodding fast again, I added "Yeah, of course it's a great idea!"

By the time I heard John laughing like crazy we were already parked and getting out. "Good, because we already set up a profile for you on multiple dating websites!"

I whipped my head toward him and shouted. "What! Why would I want that! I'm not ready for that! I don't want a relationship."

John looked back at me as he pushed the elevator button. "Henrick, you're my best friend and I know you better than you know yourself. You want this. You'll thank me after your date tonight with a girl named, Lily"

I fumbled for the second time the day trying to figure out how to get out of this. "She sounds like she likes yellow! What if she wears it on the date!"

John rolled his eyes and replied, "Well, the likelihood of that is very low and anyways you'll find out at five when you meet her at Toni's."

Toni's was my favorite restaurant. Toni was extremely understanding about my Xanthophobia and made sure there was no yellow in the dishes he makes. There isn't even yellow in the restaurant! I grumbled a bit, "Fine, I'll try."

John smiled big and exclaimed, "Good! You have one hour till you must be there! Let's get a move on."

I fidgeted in my seat as I stared at the girl across from me, or mainly the yellow dress she was wearing. As she continued to speak about herself, she scoffed, "Um, my eyes are up here you creep."

I snapped my eyes up to meet her angry ones. I stuttered "U-Um y-yeah I know yellow. I mean Lily. That's just such a nice dress we don't want to get it dirty."

Dang it John, low likelihood my butt. I grabbed all of cloth napkins and started to tuck them onto her dress, trying to cover the most yellow I could. She scoffed again and slapped me, getting up from the table and leaving immediately after. Well that went well. As she stormed out throwing the cloth napkins on the ground as she went, Toni walked over and remarked "Well, that wasn't the best date I've seen at my restaurant. Are you all right, Henry?"

I nodded and slouched into the chair. "Yeah, thanks for asking Toni. Can I have one of your burgers, no cheese or mustard?"

Toni smiled and nodded "Of course kid. On the house for my favorite customer."

I smiled and said thank you, zoning out again as he left. I finished my burger and left after talking to Toni for about twenty minutes. I was now just walking around. The air was crisp and cold, the best thinking weather. I walked over to the pharmacy that was only about a half an hour walk from Toni's with my thinking pace, wearing my sunglasses even when there was no sun to be seen. I found out sunglasses do well to cover the color of yellow, not perfect but good. People keep looking at me, I guess sunglasses indoors isn't completely normal. I made It to the desk with no line pushing the bell as someone walked over and smiled.

"Hello Henrick, how have you been?" I gave a small smile back to be polite

"I have been doing okay, Jalyn. I'm here for my new prescription from Dr. Manostu, it should be in now."

She smiled and went back to grab it handing it to me saying, "Well I hope these help Henrick."

I nodded and as I turned to leave, I heard her yell out "By any chance are you free on Saturday?"

In shock I agreed "Of course! Meet you at Toni's at seven!"

Dang it John really got into my head about this dating crap. I heard her giggle "See you then!"

I made it back to the apartment about twenty minutes later and flopped on the couch for a few minutes. "I hate this"

I mumbled as I stood up and walked to the kitchen reading the orange bottle. Okay so one every morning and one every night. That's not too hard, I can do that. I opened the bottle and screamed, throwing the bottle, making pills go everywhere. Yellow. They are all freaking yellow! John came running in with his baseball bat a minute later. "What! What is it Henrick! Is someone in here?"

He exclaimed. Before I answered he looked to the ground at all the pills and started laughing hysterically. "Man, Henrick, remind me to high five Dr. M when I drop you off tomorrow. This is priceless!"

I huffed, keeping my eyes closed. "First the girl wears a yellow dress, then Jalyn asks me out and now this! Can you help with this?"

He started laughing even more wheezing in response, "She w-wore a yellow dress!"

I kept my eyes closed as I went to the floor picking up any pills I could, yelling "Not funny! Can I get some help now!"

Suddenly I heard rustling around and pill bottle tapping my hand "Here's the bottle man. Let's get these up."

I smiled, keeping my eyes closed still.

It took about ten minutes to get all the pills off the floor counting the few times John laughed while I explained my day to him. "That is so weird. Jalyn asked you out?"

We were both sitting on the couch now talking about everything still. "Yeah, why is that weird?"

He chuckled responding, "Well its weird because when have you guys really talked other than 'Oh Henrick here are your pills' and 'Thanks' I just can't remember any time you guys talked outside of the pharmacy, that's all."

I laughed back and wiggled my eyebrows, "I just have that undeniable charisma and charm, I guess. Girls can't handle it."

We both laughed together as he responded "Yeah, that is definitely it."

I smiled and thought of Jalyn. A girl I had known for years. A girl who I talked to during her every lunch break. A friend.

We both walked out of the car after an hour drive to Dr. Manostu's office. We both walked up to the door and John stopped saying in a motherly voice, "Well sweetie I'm going to go to the store, I'll pick you up right after school is over."

We both laughed for a second before I walked into the office giving a short wave to him as I went in completely with Dr. Manostu waiting. "Well, hello Henrick. How are you doing?"

He welcomed as I sat down on the chair. I kept a straight, non-smiling face as I replied, "Am I a joke to you?"

Dr. Manostu's face went serious when he addressed "I didn't realize asking how you are meant I was treating you like a joke, Mr. Lawson."

I rolled my eyes "The pills, doctor. They were yellow."

Dr. Manostu looked at me and grinned "Well, Henrick, the best way to learn to swim is to just toss you out there. So, in order to help get over this Xanthophobia we must introduce a little bit of yellow at a time. Those pills will help you be able to live a normal or at least semi-normal life."

I nodded in response. I guess that makes sense, a little bit. "I'm doing well then. I actually have a date tonight with Jalyn."

Dr. Manostu smiled "That's very good Henrick! She is a wonderful young lady."

I nodded and fidgeted with my hands. Dr. Manostu looked at my hands "Henrick, you have to take your pills, okay? You may leave if you have nothing else you wish to speak about. This was mainly about your medication. If any side effects happen that are to bad feel free to call me but, I mean, if they are bad an ER may be a better choice."

I chuckled, still looking at my hands, nodding.

I ended up meeting Jalyn at the pharmacy at six, as per John's recommendations and drive to Toni's for dinner. Since we both didn't look super dressed up, we decided it would be just a fun date, as friends. We walked out to her car, no sign of yellow in the car or the outside of it. So far, so good. Jaylin looked in the backseat where I was sitting looking at my feet and smiled. "So, Henrick would you like some music? We probably have enough time for one song before we get there."

I nodded and she turned up the music to hear two people talking on some radio show. "-And that was Hips Don't Lie by Shakira. Next up we have a Coldplay favorite, Yellow."

My head whipped up and I looked at Jalyn who was still looking up ahead as she smiled "This is my favorite song! Must be a sign, listening to my favorite song with my favorite person."

I looked at her for a second, her smile, the sparkle in her eyes and decided against what I wanted to do. Beg her to turn it off as the radio sang. "I swam across. I jumped across for you. What a thing to do. 'Cause you were all yellow"

She looked back smiling "Did you know yellow is the color of hope?"

I smiled and responded "No, I did not."

She looked at me with an expression of happiness that hid a question. "What is it you want to ask?"

She smiled again sheepishly. "Well, I know of your condition and I believe us to be friends-"

I cut her off and exclaimed "Of course we're friends!"

She nodded with a smile "Good, good, well as I was wondering if you could introduce some yellow in your life. It really is a color full of happiness and hope so, I hope we can cure you of this. I promise if you agree I will be with you every step of the way."

I took a deep breath in as we parked into the parking lot and walked out of the car to the driver's side, opening the door for her. "I-I will try."

I grabbed a familiar orange bottle from my pocket and with a shaky hand opened the bottle. Jalyn's eyes grew wide as she watched me grab a yellow pill from the bottle and took it.

"Dr. Manostu said this would help me. I want to add to your promise though."

Jalyn nodded with a smile. "I want to go out with you again."

She grabbed my hand and started walking toward the door. "I'll agree to that. If you order something with yellow."

My mind begged me not to but was silenced as we walked in to be seated.

Toni's was extremely busy for some reason, so we sat for a while before getting our orders in. "So, what do you like to do for fun Henrick?"

I laughed and said, "Well I mostly just read and watch television on my special TV."

She laughed, asking, "What makes it special?"

I smiled and replied "Well, it turns every movie black and white, so I never have to miss a new movie."

She gasped "But that's a tragedy! What about all those action movies or all those horror movies? No color would change it so much! How would you feel if you could only see black and white?"

I thought about it for a second and after looking at her

decided. "Well, that would be tragic because then I would never see your beautiful blue eyes or your vibrant red hair. I would have to say that would be tragic."

She blushed looking down for a second then quickly composed herself. "Then it's decided! Our next date will be having a movie marathon, in color."

I smiled and right as I was about to say something Toni walked up. "Well if it isn't my favorite customer. Oh, and a beautiful lady friend! What can I get for you today?"

Jalyn looked at the menu one last time. "I will have the wild salmon burger with a side of salad."

I looked at Jalyn, then Toni and made the best decision of my life. "I will have the usual but with cheese and mustard."

Journey to the Moon

By Isabella Dintino (Finalist)

"I cannot help but notice that you have been here for a while. Do you require assistance getting to your destination?"

When I take a seat next to you in the empty moon terminal, you turn your face away from the glass windows and look at me for the first time since you first appeared two days ago. Working at Space Transport X Terminal, I have seen an interesting array of creatures. I have stared into the solid diamond eyes of a gentleman from Neptune, looked through the vapor body of a woman returning to Jupiter, but the glowing blue stars scattered across your cheeks and nose are unlike anything I have ever seen.

"I am very tired," you answer and I am surprised to see that you are crying, misty tears blurring the stars on your cheeks. "I wish for my journey to be over."

I nod along sympathetically. "I understand," I say, and adjust my uniform to be more comfortable. "I see hundreds of people every day, all going to different places within our galaxy and beyond. I've talked to people coming from Earth and going to Mars, but I've also talked to people coming from Venus and going to HIP 13044 b, a planet in the Andromeda galaxy. Everyone's journey is long and hard, but everyone gets where they are meant to be eventually."

You stare at me for a long moment, tears still falling from iridescent eyes. I wonder what you have seen that has made such a young soul feel so ancient.

"What I'm trying to say," I continue, turning away and looking up at the sky above us. The Sun is very large here. We are so close that you can see the sunspots and faculae dancing within the chromosphere. The heat seeping through the glass above us feels magnificent on my skin. "Is that you will get to the moon in due time."

"I wish I could stay here," you muse, lower lip jutting out in a pout. "It is nice here."

I can't help but scoff. "Continue on to the moon, dear. You don't want to stay here."

You cock your head to the side, icy locks of hair falling in front of your face. "Why not?"

I keep my eyes trained on the Sun. The heat no longer feels pleasant. Instead, it feels suffocating. I take a deep breath and turn back to you.

"It is not nice to not have a place to go home to," I explain quietly, reluctantly. "This is merely a stop for travelers, a place to rest and rekindle. This is not the destination."

Realization dawns in your pearly eyes, and I fear I have said too much.

"Where are you from?" You ask me, although I get the feeling you already know.

I sigh and it carries along with it the weight of all of my regrets and shame. I raise one scorched hand to the ceiling, flattening my palm to the glass. My skin instantly absorbs the heat and I relish in the feeling that is similar to cupping a steaming mug between frozen hands.

"I am from the Sun," I answer, remorse hanging off my shoulders like a cloak. "But I cannot live there."

This time, when I look back at you, you are also staring at the sun. The reds and oranges blend beautifully into the gray-silver of your iris'.

"Much like how I cannot live on Pluto," you sympathize. "At least not anymore."

I try to imagine Pluto in my head, a desolate place created of ice and snow and loneliness. I wonder which part made you want to leave. I do not ask.

"Why do you stay here if it is not a home?" You ask, interrupting my thoughts. "You said so yourself that this is not the destination."

For a question that I ask myself every day, I am suddenly not prepared to answer it. "I...I don't know," I reply truthfully. I always thought of this place as temporary, after all, it is just work. But now I'm starting to think the only reason I've stayed here for as long as I have is that I have nowhere else to go. I cannot go back to the Sun. It almost destroyed me at birth.

"Come to the moon with me," you exclaim, clasping your hands in front of you in a pleading gesture. "Or go to Earth. Just travel with me."

My chest tightens at the mere suggestion. Leave? Travel? Go to the moon with a stranger I just met?

"Please," you continue. "I don't want to go alone."

"But you don't know me," I find myself arguing half-heartedly. "And I don't know you."

"Well, you know I am from Pluto and I'm traveling to the moon. You know that I am very tired and need help finishing my journey. And I know you are from the Sun, but you couldn't stay there because it hurt you too much. And I know you work here at the Space Transport X Terminal. And I know you want to leave because this is just a stop, not the destination." You lay the facts out in front of me like a finished puzzle, with all the pieces right where they belong.

I shake my head, a shadow of a smile trying to creep across my face. Reluctantly, I let it. I meet your eyes, suddenly finding comfort in the chill that runs down my spine when I do. Cold is something my fiery skin is not used to.

"But I still don't know your name," I say. "If we were to travel together, what would I call you?"

"Eira," you say and I watch in awe as pale blue blush blooms over your cheeks. "You may call me Eira."

I nod, tasting the word on my tongue before I spoke it. It tasted sugary sweet, like ice cream from Earth. "Okay, Eira. You can call me Sulien."

No Matter What

By Lauryn Bickle (Finalist)

Someone once asked me

What day I would relive

Without changing a thing.

That would be the day I met you

Because that day was followed

By so many others I often replay.

Even when times were though

I wouldn't change a moment-

It got us here.

""Here"" is colored

With pages of memories, but

It is all I have left of you.

Most nights I walk

Down memory lane

To find you all over again,

You don't have to be my home,

But you will always have one in my heart.

R&R: Rice and Relationships

By Isabel Marie S. Auclair (Finalist)

"Nanay, sing me that song again." Mama puts down her iPad for graphic design and looks over her glasses at me. Her white hair makes her brown skin even darker.

"The one about planters in the rice fields?" Mama doesn't have an accent anymore, but I can tell the Tagalog is hovering just behind her tongue, waiting to come out.

I nod. "The one that goes, 'magtanim ay di biro'."

Mama huffs when I sit down next to her, nudging her sideways until we both fit on the chair. "I'll tell you a story instead. When Filipinos on the rice terraces plant rice and harvest rice, what is it called?"

"Hmm, I dunno." I push my face into her shoulder until her arm lifts over my head and settles around me.

"It's called palay, because the rice is still husked. Then

the rice is husked and put in bags and brought to supermarkets. When we buy the rice in bags, what is it called?"

"Rice?" Mama sighs, and I laugh.

"Hindi, anak. It's bigas, because the rice is husked but not cooked yet. Then we bring the rice home and wash it, and measure it out and cook it in the rice cooker. When we eat our rice, what is it called?"

"Good!" This time Mama laughs.

"Yes, anak, it is good. But it's called kanin, because we can now eat the rice that came all the way from the rice terraces."

"Nanay, I miss Barney."

Rolling her eyes, Mama taps my shoulder playfully. "Dios ko! You're in college next year and you're sad over a mini rice cooker?"

I sit up from where I'd settled comfortably. "Nanay, Barney was my childhood! I wanted to take Barney to college with me!"

"And you called it Barney. We could as easily have called it 'eggplant'. It's the same color."

"It's not the same!"

Mama eyes me with an eyebrow lifted. "Hindi?"

I pinch my mouth shut and look away from her sharp eyes. I knew it was just a rice cooker. It wasn't even big. Instead, it was really small. Only three cups of rice. But I still loved it. Our rice cooker. Barney had been awake when we were awake. Barney had slept when we slept. When we ate, Barney was always there. I had wanted to take Barney to college with me, a little taste of home in the big, wide world. But Barney died.

Mama's hand on my shoulder pulls me out of my thoughts. "Fine, fine. Stop crying. You're a big girl now, not my bunso anymore."

I feel her eyes trace my face before she sighs. "Magtanim ay di biro/ Maghapong nakayuko/ Di naman makatayo/ Di naman makaupo."

I blink multiple times. It's not an emotional song. It's not even a sad song. Magtanim ay Di Biro is a nursery rhyme about how hard planting rice is. Planting rice is not easy/ One is bent all day long/ You can't stand straight/ You can't sit properly.

"Halina, halina, manga kaliyag/

Tayo'y magsipag unat-unat/

Magpanibago, tayo ng lakas/

para sa araw ng bukas."

I laugh, or try to. "That song's so sad. I don't know why I asked you to sing it."

Mama mirrors my laugh, except hers actually sounds like a laugh. "Do you know what that last verse means, anak?" When I don't answer, she continues, "It means, 'Come on, come on, friends. Let's stretch and renew our strength, so that we're strong for tomorrow morning.' It isn't a sad song, aking bunso. It's a song that says, no matter how hard your life is today, you still have people around you that will help you take the next step forward."

Mama's hand begins to pat a lulling rhythm on my shoulder. "You're going to college soon. Living in a dorm, making new friends, meeting young men…"

"Nanay…"

"Make sure to take them to church before the first date, anak. Make sure Jesus approves."

"Nanay!"

Mama laughs. "Ay nako. You're growing up fast, and life will be hard. Just remember that there are people to lean on, oo? You're not on your own. Tell your friends, call me and tell your nanay, go to church and pray about it."

She kisses my head. "It's okay to complain. Just stretch, renew your strength, and get up the next day."

I sit with her for a long time, not really seeing what she's doing or what she's designing. Eventually my feet take me back to my room to finish my school. Dinner is kanin at ulam, the usual meat-and-rice dish that's the staple Pinoy meal. Barney is missing from the kitchen counter, instead there's a bigger, white rice cooker that's been sitting in storage for ten years. I serve myself less rice than usual, but inside think, "She looks like an 'Eva'."

I pack for college. Time passes, and I forget about the conversation in Mama's office. I apply for summer work, and audition for a summer theater program. I memorize all the faces in my choir, so I can remember them until the next break. I apply for scholarships online, and read articles about how to boost my resume.

Until one day, when spring is still cold, there's a bag on my desk. A custom-made tote bag, with a note in the classic, brusk style of all typical Asian parents.

""Don't break your back using this for everything. Use your backpack. And practice your Tagalog."

I turn over the bag and pause before pressing the back of my hand to my mouth. The words, "Palay, Bigas, Kanin" are on top of a mini rice cooker.

Socks and Crocs

By Anna Mutzenberger (Finalist)

"Ew! What are you wearing?"

That was the response I received one morning from a "friend", let's call her Julie, when I arrived at school. When I woke up and got ready for school that morning I thought I looked great. My hair was up in a clean ponytail, I had on a tie-dye t-shirt, a pair of sleek black shorts, ankle length black socks, and my brand new shiny white Crocs. I was so excited to finally show off my new Crocs. It was one of my first days at a new school, so I was still trying to make new friends and fit in. I figured Crocs are a name brand, comfortable, and a stylish shoe. Turns out not everyone believes that Crocs are as cool as I do. The problem Julie had was not with the Crocs themselves but what lie inside them. I had made, what she thought was the horrible mistake of wearing my Crocs with socks.

I believe that wearing socks with your Crocs is not wrong, but the best way to wear Crocs. Without socks, your feet rub up against the shoes and can easily cause blisters and discomfort. Not only that, but your feet stick to them and the bumps on the bottom just feel weird on bare feet.

After Julie made that horrible comment about my footwear of choice, my day was ruined. All I wanted to do was go home and throw away my brand-new pair of Crocs because they had caused all of this. But when my mom picked me up from school, she asked me what was wrong. So I decided to tell her everything that Julie had said, and that I didn't want to wear my Crocs ever again. By the time I finished my story we had just pulled into the garage and my mom said, "Before you went to school today you were so excited about your new Crocs. You shouldn't let the actions and words of someone else choose how you want to live your life. You should wear the things you like, and you should do the things you like to do. No matter what other people think of you".

That tragic day I learned a very valuable lesson. The lesson I learned was not fashion advice about socks and Crocs from Julie, but a much deeper more meaningful lesson. I learned how important it is not to let people change you. If you want to wear your Crocs with socks, do it! If you want to wear dresses every day, go for it! Wear what you want to wear. Don't dress a certain way because someone says you should, or you feel like it's the only way to fit in. Dress for yourself, even if it means upsetting Julie because you wore socks with your Crocs.

Sunday

By Rishi Makam (Finalist)

Up until middle school, I dreaded Sundays; my mom's voice echoing from the bottom of the stairs, "Get up. Brush your teeth. Take a quick shower. Hurry downstairs." After rushing through breakfast, my family and I would then begin the strenuous car ride to the place I loathed most, Sunday school. I attempted everything from faking illness to throwing a tantrum, but my lies were transparent. Nothing got me out of the four wasted hours I spent ignoring the monotonous priest.

Before classes begin, the head priest of my temple leads the Prayer Hall. We take off our shoes, find an open spot on the floor, and attempt to listen to the redundant speech that goes in one ear and out the other. About an hour passes and everyone then stands up to recite the final prayer before we head off to the main classes: religion and language. I walk as slow as I can in hopes of avoiding my inevitable fate. I get to my class five minutes late, but it's inconsequential because I still have to sit through an hour and a half of my teacher prating on about myths in Hinduism. After what feels like hours, the class ends and I get up to go to my second and last class of the day. I get to the class where we learned Telugu, my native language. I take a seat in the hard plastic chair and immediately start to daydream. I think about how learning to speak a language was more important than learning to write a language, but the teacher never focused on the speaking aspect. I snap back into reality when I realize students are beginning to leave. I follow everyone out and meet my family near the main hall where we thank the priest and leave. These classes seemed pointless and wasteful, but ultimately I realized they were exceedingly valuable to my identity.

During seventh and eighth grade, I began learning about The Bhagavad Gita. The story held within my religion's sacred text not only gave me a better understanding of my culture, but also taught me valuable life lessons. It was the first time I was ever truly captivated by what was being taught at Sunday school. My attitude towards the class completely changed. I woke up every Sunday morning full of vigor and spirit. I brought an end to my constant barrage of complaints and excuses. The once strenuous car ride to the temple became a blissful journey to a peaceful haven. The Bhagavad Gita explained the soul and how it is essential to keep it in balance in order to maintain inner peace. It also explained how living a life of altruism and empathy leads to a more satisfied well being. I apply these lessons to my life every day, and because of them, I can be my best self.

Sunday school ended when I graduated middle school. I

wanted to share what I learned in Sunday school with my peers. During my sophomore year, I was presented with the opportunity to help found a club that would do exactly that: South Asian Club. We appreciate and recognize South Asian traditions by teaching others about them and immersing others in cultural experiences. The club gained traction quickly and many members joined to learn more about the many holidays and customs in South Asia. I am now able to embrace what I have learned during Sunday School in order to teach others about what I believe in.

The Chimes

By Kayla Maura Freedman (Finalist)

Franklin pulled into the garage of the house and turned off the ignition of his old, rusty green car. He hobbled out of his seat, closed the door, and locked the doors behind him. He climbed up the steps of the house, using the railing for support. At his age, he was one fall away from death. His shaky hands reached for the knob and he flung the door wide open, peering inside. Everything was just how he left it, and yet everything felt different.

Franklin walked into the tiny bathroom near the door. His hands grasped the sides of the sink and his head slowly lifted. His eyes glared into the mirror, analyzing his reflection. His eyes were dark and empty. There wasn't a spark like there used to be. His face was wrinkly and saggy. His pruney fingers rustled through his hair, which was thin and balding. His shoulders were tense and his eyebrows were furrowed. He didn't recognize himself. It was terrifying. A tear slid down his face.

The beach house was Franklin's favorite place in the world. Franklin and Ava would travel up there every summer in that very same green car. They would sing songs and laugh until they couldn't breathe. They would ride bikes on the boardwalk and eat ice cream. Franklin loved chocolate and Ava loved vanilla. They would lounge on the beach and chase seagulls. They lived in a dream. They were perfect together. Everyone said so. It's very rare to meet your perfect soulmate in your lifetime, but Franklin and Ava had found each other.

This year, Ava passed away. Franklin didn't believe their time was coming to an end. He refused to accept it. He missed her more than anyone has ever missed anyone. She was his reason for living.

He made it out to the porch. He took in the ocean air and felt the wind shuffle through his cardigan. He carefully sat down in one of the purple chairs they had put out a few years back. He wished Ava was sitting next to him, laughing at him, teasing him, kissing him. He turned back towards the view and let out a long breath. He began to bawl. Tears and snot streamed down his face as he gripped his heart.

Suddenly, he heard the sounds of music. He looked down towards the end of the porch and saw the wind chimes. Ava found them at a market and told him that she had to have them. They moved like magic. He helped himself up and approached the windchimes. The wind made them dance and the light flowed through the glass. Franklin smiled. He let his shoulders relax and he took out his handkerchief to wipe off his tears. He leaned up against the white railing off the porch and watched the windchimes.

Franklin was calm for the first time in a long time. He was

brought back to Ava. He imagined her laughing with her mouth open and milk squirting out of her nose. He pictured her dancing with no music on. He remembered her finding the windchimes at the market and setting them up on the porch. He opened his eyes because the music had stopped. The day had become quiet and the wind had gone. He studied the still chimes. The glass was smooth and beautiful, and he realized why Ava loved them so much.

Franklin knew in his heart that Ava would never have wanted this for him. In fact, she would slap him if she saw him as depressed as he was. But as he touched the chimes, he felt closer to Ava than he had in a long time. At that moment, he began to accept she was gone. Acceptance was not a stage Franklin ever wanted to go through. But just for that split second, he lived in a state of tranquility and a state of peace. He knew it wouldn't last forever. He held onto Ava's favorite thing because she was his favorite thing. He started to cry again but it was different. The tears were filled with love, instead of pain. He was going to get through this.

The First Christmas

By Ashley Dawn (Finalist)

As the car turned into the driveway, dread overtook Kiran's tentative anticipation. Turning away from the window and back towards Mrs. Smith's babbling, Kiran nodded slightly, smiling at her in the rearview mirror.

"Well dear, thanks for chatting with me on the way home. As you can probably tell, my own daughter is already tired of me."

A side glance confirmed Mrs. Smith's suspicion as white wires dangled from Maddy's ears, spouting snippets of "Watermelon Sugar" into the cramped backseat. After running into one another at the terminal, Mrs. Smith had insisted that they drive Kiran home, shutting down all notion of Kiran taking the commuter rail. Maddy had toed the specked tiles of Logan at her mother's insistence, plugging her headphones in with a grimace. Despite the lack of texts and calls since they left for college in September, Kiran had half-expected Maddy to offer up one of the earbuds, excitedly queuing the newest songs that Kiran just had to listen to. When she hadn't, Kiran had turned to the window, noting how unfamiliar the drive home had become.

"I'll pop the trunk for you," Mrs. Smith interrupted, catching Kiran's eye and smiling weakly, in the sad way that adults always did now. "Should you go get your dad to help with your bags, dear?"

"No, I got it. I have always been a light packer!" Kiran blurted in what she hoped was a reassuring tone as she quickly unbuckled and opened the car door.

From the trunk she grasped her beaten orange duffle bag, the only thing she had brought with her to college. In August, her dad had been far too preoccupied with insurance policies and paperwork to care about drop-off day. After a solemn and stiff goodbye she had taken the train, alone, to catch her flight.

"You got everything?" Maddy's apprehensive tone interrupted the memory as she emerged from the backseat. She spoke precisely, careful not to speak too loudly or say anything out of place. Kiran hated it. She despised how Maddy avoided her as if she were about to burst at any moment.

She gathered the overstuffed bag and gave Maddy a quick nod, mumbling something about hanging out over the holidays. Maddy nodded in return, giving a slight wave as Kiran hoisted her bag to her shoulder and approached the steps of the house. The stout colonial offered little reprieve from Maddy's iciness: the yellow color, once bright and cheery, blared insincerely; the curtains, drawn over every window, concealed where candles once burned every Christmas; and the typical wreaths and garlands were conspicuously missing from where they once adorned porches and doors. Her mom had always been the first in the neighborhood to put those Christmas decorations up, eagerly awaiting the day when she could exchange her pumpkins for bells.

Kiran breathed deeply, embracing the frigid air as it burned through her body. Pushing aside the grief welling at her throat, she gave Ms. Smith a final wave, and pushed the door open. The creak echoed in the bare foyer, bouncing off walls in harmony with the moans of wooden planks as she dropped her bag heavily. Despite the warmth of the house, Kiran felt a chill run down her spine as her eyes fell over the hallway before her. "I'm home," she called hesitantly.

When no one responded, she walked to the basement door, tiptoeing as though to not interrupt the silence of her home. As she pressed her ear to the door, she heard 80s rock music faintly spilling from downstairs. For a moment she let herself go back to how things were. Leaning against the door, she closed her eyes, imagining that her dad would come upstairs lugging his newest creation: a bookshelf for the living room, or a ping pong table for her and Emily, or a chair for her mom's classroom. They'd applaud his efforts, drinking in his smell of sawdust and smoke as it mixed with the casserole mom was making for dinner.

A wet droplet fell onto Kiran's arm, startling her from the memory. She realized she was crying and quickly wiped her face with her sleeves. At school she hadn't allowed herself to cry: she had tried so hard to be okay, making friends and passing every moment with others to keep herself in check. Coming home had unleashed something in her; the past six months melted away and she was back where she started, alone and cold in an empty home.

Taking a deep breath in, she turned the knob to the basement and began the descent into the workshop, careful to avoid making eye contact with the pictures hanging on the walls. God, she couldn't understand how her dad could bear to look at them. Every day, seeing, being surrounded by memories. After only a few minutes at home, Kiran felt suffocated. She was glad she had chosen Indiana University-- somewhere far away from Concord and all that wasn't there.

She turned the corner of the staircase, knocking gingerly on the wall that led into her dad's workshop. At the sound he startled from where he sat, measuring blocks of wood and marking them with his pencil, and looked up to meet Kiran's gaze. Their eye contact was heavy, suspending grief and confusion amidst the dust particles that floated around the room. As he smiled softly, guilt flooded Kiran's body.

"I'm sorry for leaving you all alone," she managed through tears.

Her dad let out a small yelp as he crossed the room to gather her in his arms. "I'm so sorry, Kiran. I've left you alone too," he choked out through tears, holding her tightly.

For the first time they shared the weight of the past year, leaning against one another as they cried.

The Last Goodbye

By Stella Walborn (Finalist)

The smell of overwhelming disinfectants assaults my nose as I glance around the dimly lit room and find the clock once again. I squeeze your hand gently as if to pull you from the surrounding darkness that you are in. Your eyelids are closed as a machine breathes for you, how could it come to this? We were supposed to have the world ahead of us and now I can't even get you to open your eyes. Hanging my head, I cry bitterly. Couldn't we had just stayed home?

Casting my mind back, I see us together laughing and smiling about an inside joke. We were so happy, so alive. Then he approaches and asks us if we would come to his celebration he is throwing, "Just a small one, I promise". We smile, as our eyes meet, wondering if this is some shy way of asking you out. You accept for both of us, knowing, of course, we want to take advantage of this opportunity. He gives a cool nod, and a charming smile aimed in your direction and swivels his head slightly to include me. I didn't mind, we both knew you were head over heels for this boy, with the beautiful eyes and intelligent mind.

We sing at the tops of our lungs as we get dressed at your house, casual yet perfect. Searching for the ""right"" look among the racks of clothes in your closet. For the 20th time, I tease you about your cute freckles and you respond with your usual, "Maybe they'll disappear one day". Pulling on our sporty, matching Nike sneakers, we give each other "the look", making sure we do indeed look perfect for the event. Satisfied, we clutch each other's hands in anticipation, my eyes glowing with excitement for you! How I wish, I could have known what was to come and even faked an illness so you wouldn't go.

Pulling up in your sleek BMV, we enter the driveway with a few other cars. Loud music plays from the house and it sets the mood for the night. You wink at me and promise that this will be a night to remember for both of us. You were so right, as you usually were, yet I've wished a thousand times that you were not. I nod, and we enter the Victorian-style house. He greets us with the same brilliant smile taking in our outfits. I guess we both passed inspection as he opened the door, but leaned over to you and asked if he could show you the gardens. Blushing, you replied, "Well, of course!". We walked in together greeting our friends that were already there enjoying the food and music. I spotted one of my closest friends from the lab and motioned that you should take him up on his offer now. How many times have I wished to take that moment back? Too many to count.

I see you head out the patio door and I see him greet you and take your hand. I smile, thinking that you make the perfect couple. Heading over to my friend, we grab some food and find a place to talk about the group project that is due in a week. I smile as I recall, you saying that I am all business even at gatherings. Time passes quickly, and as we stand up to refill our plates, I notice the grey clock hanging on the wall, approaching 10 o'clock. I remember the promise you made to your mom, to always be home my ten. Waving to my friend I explain I must go. I open the side door and look for you. The gardens are empty, with a slight breeze creating goosebumps on my skin. Odd, I think, but decide you must have gotten chilly and went inside. I ask around, no one has seen you or him. My natural fear instinct kicks in, but I calm myself down as I dial your number. My heart rate escalates as it goes right to voicemail.

Suddenly, we all hear this terrific crash as his Dodge Charger rips through the side of the house. I scream, horrified for him, forgetting that you are missing. Reality strikes, as I see a flash of copper hair and recognize the T-shirt of the person in the passenger seat, it's you. People are moving around me frantically. Someone calls 911, but I am frozen to the floor. It seems like a bad movie; how could this happen so quickly? As the ambulance and police arrive, I slowly compose myself and answer their questions. Numbly, I answer their questions and nod stiffly. Was it a large party? No. Do you know anyone? Yes. Why did you come? I shrug my shoulders, and answer weakly, "She liked him". The injuries are bad, they call your mom, and I can hear her hysterical words and utterances on the other side of the phone.

Now it's been only 10 hours since the shocking accident.

Your skin is pale and your hair is spread out like a fan behind you, a sharp color contrast. Your mom is sitting with me, her beautiful face frozen with concern. She looks at me with slightly veiled anger, and I cannot blame her. It will take a miracle for you to awake from your coma. He has died instantly, but you were lucky, you remembered your seatbelt which saved you from crashing through the windshield. I wish I could have told him no, we weren't interested in going. Convinced you that he wasn't your type. Regrets fly through my mind faster and faster. Lifting my swollen eyes, I glance at your still form again and shudder uncontrollably. Getting up softly, I kiss your forehead, in case this is the last goodbye.

What Life is Really About

By Sophia (Finalist)

It was 7 pm on a Thursday. I glanced out the window, and remember having no connection to myself. How did everyone except me have their life together? Why couldn't I be perfect as everyone else? My mother walked into the kitchen and asked me "Do you want to drink chai?" At that time, I had no idea what she said. I simply said "yes" because I was too mentally exhausted to listen to what she was saying.

My mother set the chai in front of me. I had never tried chai before, but I told myself to try it. I'll never forget the heavenly flavor that my tastebuds felt when I took the first sip. It was sweet, yet it had an undertone of pistachio and rose to add tanginess. I knew that I had to learn how to make this drink. Little did I know, learning this skill was my first step to gaining a realistic perspective of the world.

At fifteen years old, I expected myself to be perfect like a robot that never made mistakes. To many people, Chai is just tea. However, making chai helped my naive younger self realize what life was truly about. When you make chai, it can be awful or great. There's no in-between. The first sip of my mother's chai was absolutely amazing. The first time I made it, it was awful. It was nothing like my mother's. I thought there was something personally wrong with me, and felt discouraged.

However, something inside of me wouldn't let go of hope to make delicious chai. At the time I couldn't define what that longing was. Not wanting to lose hope for that connection again, I decided to keep trying.

I kept trying for weeks, but my chai still tasted absolutely awful. I was so confused. It wasn't until the sixth week when I finally realized what I was doing wrong. I was trying the same failed method every day, and expecting better results each time. Similarly, I was expecting stellar life results when none of the habits I had at the time-correlated with good results. It finally clicked. I had to try new methods of making chai so that I could learn through process and experience.

Over the next few weeks, I conducted research to see how other people made chai and applied those new methods to my routine every day. I added cardamom and vanilla extract to give it flavor, and cinnamon for the ginger taste. Similarly, I did research on healthy sleep habits and studying effectively.

My chai finally started tasting better. The flavor was more heightened, and I gained more experience. Similarly, in life, I was sleeping 7 hours a day, and I was starting my work immediately after school. My life was starting to improve now that I had better habits.

I lost track of how many months it took for my chai to finally taste great. All I remember is one day sitting down, with my chai in front of me, and the drink tasted heavenly. It felt better drinking my mother's chai for the first time because it was something I worked to accomplish. No longer a naive freshman, I couldn't help but realize what that feeling was the first time I tried chai. It was a connection to the way the world truly works. Life isn't about being perfect. It was okay to make mistakes as long as I applied them to my future. I learned patience. Just like making chai, life is a process that you have to learn from in order to get the end result you desire. Now, whenever life gets rough, I remind myself that the whole point of life is growing and putting in the work that it takes to get the end result you desire.

Even today, as I drink my chai, I marvel at how something as simple as a beverage taught me that new chapters of life warrant mistakes and growth. Thanks to chai, I learned that process and imperfections are key aspects to navigating through the painful and beautiful journey we call life.

SECTION 4 – MYSTERY

Desert of the Lost

By Adriane Navolis (Finalist)

Pilot's log: Day 1

The crash was horrendous, I could smell burning, feel the nausea in my gut as my aircraft tumbled through the sky. The jarring impact, then nothingness. I'm not entirely sure what happened. I am awake now, but all I can do is sit here, surrounded by wreckage. I am not sure how to react. Overall, I just feel complete and utter numbness. There is a metal taste in my mouth, and my ears are ringing. Beyond that assurance that I do indeed exist, I feel no prompting of what to do with that information.

Day 2

After a day of collecting my thoughts, I now have a solid grasp on yesterday's occurrences. On Monday morning, 8:15 am, my plane crashed into the desert. This appears to have been due to a severe malfunction in the engine. This is certainly no cause for concern as I sent out a mayday a few hours ago. My team will be here soon to rescue me. In the meantime, I will remain by the site of the wreckage, and investigate if there is any chance of bringing the craft back into functionality. The weather so far is unpleasantly hot, but I believe the radio still works, so I will call out hourly to try to reach my crew. Surely they must be nearby, they wouldn't leave me behind!

Day 3

Despite the radio miraculously still working, it has been over 24 hours with no response. All there is here is the unbearable sun at day, and freezing temperatures at night. My crew must have abandoned me for dead, blast them all! Now I am stuck here, in the middle of nowhere, with little to no rations, a useless scrap pile of a plane, and no chance of survival. Do they not even wonder what happened to me? Will they tell my family that I'm dead? Well here I am! Alive and starving away with no one to know! Why am I even writing in this forsaken journal? All that's left of it will be buried by the sand, just like I will, due to a mere engine failure. Curse my fate!

Day 4

I saw a silhouette on the horizon this morning. After calling out for what felt like a few minutes, it disappeared. Perhaps it was someone going to get help, and if I wait a little longer they will come by and bring me to safety! In other news, I believe I may have found a way to get the plane working again. The motor appears to have been damaged in the impact, but while dismantling the radio, I found a piece that if I work over enough might be just what it takes to get the whole thing running, more or less. I made certain to make several final calls with my radio before taking it apart, but perhaps this sacrifice is what it will take to get away from this barren land of emptiness.

Day 5

Completely useless. The attempt to fix the engine blew up in my face, completely ruining any other salvageable parts within the craft. Not only that, but now that my radio is gone, there is no chance of making it to the outside world. The destruction that occurred when attempting to start up the engine left me with several wounds I have not treated yet. Why bother? I am out of water, and the food supplies are not far behind. I see new mirages in the horizon each day, but calling out has only given me a dryer throat. I have let go of the hope that any of my visions are real. This is it. I will never see the faces of my family again. I will die here, and fade away into nothingness. I am completely helpless to the fact nothing is left out here to save me. All that is left to do is wait for death to take me.

Day 6

When I opened my eyes today, I encountered the strangest thing. At first I was certain it was another illusion brought by the desert heat, but it did not disappear after looking away. Upon reaching out to it my hand met short, coarse fur, confirming that the image before me was no apparition of fantasy, but indeed a dog. A dog that had somehow located me in the middle of the desert. Bewildered by this oddity, I stood. The beast backed away at the movement, and gave a bark. I took a shaky step forward, then another, my voice too hoarse to attempt speaking to it. The creature ran off a few more feet, then turned around, almost willing me to follow it. So, mustering my remaining strength, I did. At this rate, any option is better than wasting away in a wrecked plane. I will follow up again when I can with what comes of this venture.

Day 7

I had followed the dog as long as I could before my weakness overtook me, causing me to collapse. I am not entirely sure how, but upon reawakening, I was in a village! My best guess is the dog must've led its owner to me. Upon awakening, I was unsure if anything was real, despite the pain of my injuries and burns, which was actually reduced drastically. Upon further observation, and my mind clearing a little, I noticed that my wounds had been treated, and some of my supplies recovered. Later on, a woman approached me, whom I presume to be the owner of the dog, who came bounding in as well. I do not recognize her language, but even so, I must make an effort to show my gratitude. For now, although I do not know if I will ever see home again, I have new hope ahead of me. And that, beyond all else, gives me a reason to keep going.

Do You Have the Time, Sir?

By Adriana L. Robinson (Finalist)

It was quiet in the evening, it rarely ever wasn't. The night brought with it a reminder that time was always passing. It's supposed to be a clock's job to tell you when the seconds turn into minutes, not the night's. I don't own any clocks, I don't like their ticking. All they do is tic, tic, tic. There is never a moment of silence when around a clock, and yet, even in the dead silence of the night, the seconds could be heard ticking away.

It was cold in the evening, it rarely ever wasn't. The chill would bring with it the reminder that time was always ticking away. Another cold night would then lead to a slightly warmer day before once again becoming a night as frigid as the one before. It was supposed to a clock's job to tell the time, not the cold's, and I didn't own any clocks. Yet still, even in the dead silence of the night, the seconds could be heard, ticking away.

It was lonely in the evening, it rarely ever wasn't. The absence of life brought with it a reminder that time was always moving forward. The square in which I would often find myself sitting in would eventually fill with bustling people, some shopping, some hauling off to work, and some, merely just watching the world around them. It was supposed to be a clock's job to relay the hour, not the solitude's, but somehow, even in the dead silence of the night, the seconds could be heard, ticking away.

It was always the same in the evening, except for when it wasn't. It happened only once. The constant sameness I knew so well was interrupted suddenly by a man's voice.

"Do you have the time, sir?" The man stood to the side of me. He wore a well pressed suit and held a briefcase, and his eyes were trained on me expectantly.

"Well that depends on what time you're asking for." At this, the man awkwardly shuffled his feet and cleared his throat.

"I'm asking for the current time." His gaze implied urgency was curious.

"It's late." I gazed away from him, taking in the barely lit plaza. There was a fountain in the middle of the square that my eye would frequently wander to, this time was no different. The tight embrace under the umbrella. The water streamed from the top of the umbrella, making it look like the couple were really in the middle of a rainstorm. I was envious of them, their time was forever preserved in stone, unlike mine.

"I'm aware that it's late, but do you know exactly what time it is?" The man asked again as his jaw worked, clenching and unclenching, waiting for my response.

"I don't own any clocks." His brows furrowed.

"So you don't have the time then?"

"Who's to say I don't have the time?" The man shook his head and blew out a small breath.

"But you just said that you don't own any clocks."

"I don't like clocks." His eyes once again flicked down to his case then back up to me.

"Look man, I just need to know if you've got the time or not!"

"Do you?" I asked.

"What?"

"Do you have the time?" He looked at me, completely baffled. I went on. "One second after the next, time is going by and you're using yours to talk to an old man about the very thing that you're losing."

"What do you mean?" His jaw clenching and aggravated twitching stopped.

"Simply that life is lived on a schedule that we don't have the means to understand. My time could be up any minute from now, but so could yours." I finally met the man's gaze. "So let me ask you again, do you have the time, sir?"

He left without another word after I'd said that to him. Whether he was upset or intrigued, I couldn't tell. After all it was supposed to be a clock's job to have the time, not mine, and I don't own any clocks because I don't like them. Even so, hearing my time ticking away in the dead silence of the night makes me wonder if maybe, getting a clock would be quieter.

Evil, Senseless, Inhumane, Remorseless

By Maddox Umholtz (Finalist)

"Evil, senseless, inhumane, remorseless."

Rich words from a judge. In my time of infamy, I've been spat on, tackled, and had assassination attempts on my life. No action or spoken words got under my skin as much as those four words. Reason being, it completely disregards what our justice system is about. The truth. The Judge was too caught up in doing a show and being the hero that he overlooked the truth. He didn't understand the urges I resisted. He didn't understand how hard I fought and if I was a weaker man, how much worse the situation would have been. Every time, the urge would creep in, like a house centipede scuttling into a home. If your quiet enough you can hear it, but you won't see it until it's on top of you. Now one understood that so, on the day of my sentencing, I was the most human out of all of them. When a fate was given to me, they all cheered and hugged. Tears of joy ran down their faces. Where's the humanity in that? Of course, I can't be too mad at the crowd's reaction. They've been coerced into believing a false reality presented to them by the court. The theatrics and the 'yellow journalistic' prosecution perpetuated the misinformation in the crowd. The truth is so much more complicated which I can only explain with a story.

Back in 1987, It was a summer night, and I was walking down Clineville Road. I grew up on that road and I never lived anywhere else. It was a nice community where kids would run wild and there was no curfew. I saw silhouettes run under streetlights and heard, in the distance, laughter and shoes skid on gravel. There were playgrounds down every side street and back yard, making it a perfect place to be raised. I sat down at one of the many park benches' and begin with my daydreaming routine. Not being thoroughly satisfied with my place in life I found these walks quite therapeutic and a place where I can plan for the future, even if few plans come to fruition.

After about 30 minutes of sitting and thinking, a young lady I didn't recognize, burst out of one of the nearby houses, limped over and sat right next to me reeking of booze. This is one of the biggest misconceptions spread about me. The idea that I 'preyed on' or 'hunted'. I found that being gifted with good looks made me a very approachable person. I never set out to meet the lady's I meet. They always come to me first. She had red hair, a flower blouse, and was very attractive. It took me a second to realize that she was crying. Mascara ran down her cheeks and her bottom lip jittered. This vulnerable state and drunkenness probably greatly influenced her confidence because it wasn't long before she started giving me her whole life story. I found this to be especially annoying because her words were constantly being disrupted by slurring and weeping, and she wouldn't stop stuttering.

She kept saying 'I feel so betrayed' but I never got any of the context. I was too focused on her hazel eyes which kept looking at her feet and up ahead of her. Never directly at me. That's when I felt the urge. It itched behind my eyes and tickled my throat. It felt like sharp shards of ice were clogging all my veins, creating a slowly intensifying, numbing pain. My leg began to shake. She must have noticed and interpreted it as impatience.

"I'm sorry, I don't know why... I...", She cut herself off before she began to stand up. I decided to test myself and see if I could resist my urges, so I grabbed her hand.

"No, don't be sorry, please... I need the company", I said, pushing my eyebrows together to give a more sympathetic or caring look. She slowly sat back down and didn't speak. Her silence was deafening, and I became paranoid. Does she know who I am? Does she know my power? The ice in my veins grew, shattering and puncturing my viscera. The pain encapsulated my chest. My heart pounded harder as I denied my primal instincts and continued to sit in her presence quietly. The seconds scraped by and the only sound she made was the occasional sniff. I came up with an idea. I was going to rest my arm around her back. A kind gesture that expresses compassion and comfort. Maybe I can handle it.

I began by slowly lifting my arm an inch at a time. My forehead was sweating, and my muscles ached. As I was getting closer and closer the pain in my chest was becoming more and more extreme. I started to grit my teeth and shake uncontrollably. My hand was already behind her head and almost to her shoulder, when unexpectedly she rested her head on my shoulder first. My fist tightened and I froze. I stared at my fist as my nails dug in, causing blood to leak out of my palm. I was overwhelmed and the ice consuming my body began to tear the skin. The pain became incomparable, so I lurched forward and vomited between my feet. I quickly got up, walked away and didn't look back.

Would an evil man bleed and torture himself for self-betterment? Would a senseless man with all humanity lost, present a shoulder for a stranger to cry on? Would a cruel man attempt a comforting embrace? But none of that matters now. With an apple as my last meal, I choose to face the Devil on an empty stomach to show him my resistance to his temptations are strong.

Just Corn

By Katelyn Carafelli (Finalist)

It wasn't that he was dumb, he just kept finding himself in these kind of situations. Three AM, miles from the nearest hint of civilization, and his car was minutes away from running out of gas. Milo, an amateur photographer, had been searching for an abandoned barn to photograph. It turned out that the barn had been torn down to make room for more farmland; however, he realized this way too late and was undeniably lost in the rolling hills.

Surrounding him on all sides, was endless corn fields, stretching for as far as the eye could see. The night was incredibly dark, not even the moon nor stars shown through the gloomy black. The deserted one lane road he was traveling down did nothing more but add to his paranoia. With every inch his car rolled down the rocky path, something within the corn seemed to stalk him. The corn shifted in the corner of his eye as he drove, but everytime he turned towards it, the movement vanished.

Milo shuddered, and instinctively began to fiddle with the buttons of his car. Soon enough cheery music was blasting through the speakers. But not even pop could calm his nerves. Although, he was surprised he even was in range of a station at this point. His last contact with humanity had been at a gas station 20 miles from where he was now. Throughout the whole experience, the store had been empty. Not a soul in the dimly lit and vaguely bleach smelling building except for the ancient cashier woman, whose eyes narrowed with his every move. They definitely didn't like outsiders here.

His car, old, dented, and struggling with almost every movement, bumped along the dusty road. He peered into the darkness searching for any kind of road sign indicating he was at least approaching something. But between the brown curls falling in his face, his glasses, and the black of night, he saw absolutely nothing. Nothing but endless corn. Losing his general optimistic spirit, Milo sighed and pulled over to the side of the road and killed the engine. With a few clicks, the glove compartment popped open. He rummaged through numerous college textbooks and receipts before finding the maps he was looking for. He opened and sprawled one across the dashboard and began looking for the town he had come from.

Just as he recognized his location on the map, his car lurched. A heart wrenching metal screech blared from what seemed like all around him. The car seemed to tip onto its side and let out a variety of noises expressing its disregard for the situation. Milo yelped and grabbed onto the seat trying not to be slammed into the other end of the car. He felt the awful pull of gravity as he was lifted into the air, dangling from the seat. As the car began to tilt back to its original position, he instinctively dived and cowered under his seat and piles of maps. But then, silence. It seemed whatever it was, had passed.

With shaky hands, Milo fumbled for the car door and stepped out in order to survey the damage. The entire left side of his car had been destroyed. Gigantic claw marks, a singular stroke, spanned the entire length of his car. Milo's heart dropped. What could've done that? Kansas was once home to animals like cougars and grizzly bears, but they had long since been exterminated. He looked around the area. No movement, no sign anything had been there. Just corn.

But the hair on the back of his neck began to rise. Something was there, watching his every move. With a sudden sense of panic and dread, Milo ran towards the driver's seat. But the thing was faster. He was instantly overwhelmed by something much bigger than him. He couldn't see it as he tried to scramble his way out of its clutches, but claws, the size of corn husks, gouged into his arms and hauled him backwards. Milo dug his hands into the rocky ground in a desperate attempt to escape, but his efforts were useless. He was dragged into the corn, pieces of stalk piercing his skin and clothes. He screamed and fought with all his ability, but in seconds it was all over. He was gone. Vanished into the corn.

A couple of miles down the road sat another car. Empty with doors open. A few miles further, there was another. But the night was quiet. There was nothing. Just corn.

Mysterious Puppeteers

By Evelynn Esparza (Finalist)

A soft glow of orange emits from the darkness of what looked to be the void. You reach your hand out for the new source of light, once you come into contact with it, you could feel the warmth and the new found determination within you. Appearing in a place filled with strangers for each room you enter, and engaging in many battles only to die over and over again till it's insufferable. Saving was the only thing you could do in order to save your progress, but each time you find yourself back where you died with the new feeling of determination inside of your soul. you must continue till the end... Each journey will lead to you finding friends and a new love... a ""happy"" ending. Once the story ends you begin your journey again, only to repeat itself over and over again, the same dialogue.. the same battles... and befriending people who don't remember you. Growing bored and tired of the same happy ending... what if you wanted to do something new, something different, the only route you followed was a pacifist one, so why not receiving more dialogue by... choosing different paths, if it doesn't work out then you could always start over again with everyone forgetting who you were with only being left with a sense of dejavu, you slowly realized the power you possessed and were dubbed a megalomaniac. Whatever choice you made had no consequences or so it seems.. This story has been told by many people, just different variations... how about we make our own story, one that makes you cheer for a character, and weep for another while there is no happy ending.

"We think of ourselves as gods when we create our ideas, our own little worlds where we are able to do as we please without any consequences. Each person is different, their actions and morals can be different compared to others. WE create, WE cause characters to suffer, WE give characters a motive, everything we do can be projected to a character that can be used for a story. Every bad ending and every happy ending a character receives is all up to us... I am here to invite every curator who is willing to join in this new story that will for sure put everyone on the edge of their seats!" a maniacal laughter could be heard after and slowly dissipated to silence... a message for creators and a start of a new story that could turn into chaos or possibly a war.

No one thought of joining for they feared for the worst, but the ones that weren't scared and had a background of making genocidal stories, or even inevitable sad endings have accepted the invitation and with that... an association was formed called "puppeteers". It didn't take long for them to use their own favorite characters as pawns in their game of chess. Controlling them against their own wills, forcing the characters to travel throughout the fictional multiverses only to wreak havoc. The one who didn't participate was none other than the one invited them, who was now dubbed as "Narrator". They were the brains of the operation and no one knew what they were capable of and what they had in store for the audience. They may have godly powers over a fictional world, but there are limitations... it was like a videogame, each character had status', showing their health, attack and defense. They can't revise their character's for they have already been published and set, their character's limitations are the creator's limitations in controlling them.

"You each have now received masks to hide your true identities, each different from the others, now choose the name you will go by throughout our adventure together?" The voice rang throughout a spatial themed room that only had a table with eight empty seats while on the end is none other than the narrator as each creator has been given a black and white mask with only emotes on them. "You may take a seat once you have chosen, and welcome to the spatial room, where no one will disturb our purge of plot." It was easy to tell the Narrator had a sinister look under their mask, but no one pointed this out.. This is where it all begins, but with bad there is always good around the corner.

One Last Time

By Kendahl Parsons (Finalist)

She gripped the handle of her black iron blade and continued forward.

"One last time," she muttered to herself.

One last time. That's what she had said the time before, and the time before that. The truth was that there was no "one last time," not for her. There was no way out of this mess, no way without death, that is. The way of her world was kill or be killed. It wasn't right. In fact, it was very wrong. It shouldn't have been the cruel reality that it was. But the real problem was that she didn't mind killing, sure, the first couple had hurt, but it didn't affect her anymore. That was the cruelest thing about the situation. She had grown up killing, killing wasn't what bothered her. It was the loneliness. It was the loneliness that gnawed at her heart, taunted her. But it was the only thing keeping her human. It was because of her job, she was forced to live in the shadows, only appearing to kill.

She had been selected from her village at a young age by the king himself. At the time, she had been grateful to be picked by the king himself for such an important job. Now she knew better. In reality, she had been plucked by a controlling dictator out of what had been a happy life with her family. He had destined her to a life of service. She was no more than a slave. She could barely remember her parents. Her only memory is of her parents thoughtlessly taking fortune over her. It was clear she was wanted nowhere, belonged nowhere. Maybe it was better that way. The world was a cruel place.

Yet, she desperately longed for someone to talk to, to laugh with, someone to share the burdens with. But with her vow to serve, she also vowed to be forever alone. She shook her head, as if trying to shake the foolish thoughts away. Her wishes did not matter in her career if you could even call it that. She just had to get the job done and move on to the next. Despite the facts, she still promised to herself, one last time. This would be the last time she killed. She needed a new life, before her heart turned as cold as the rest of her. Before it was too late.

She continued walking down the worn path, the wet rocks crunching under her boots. She saw a flicker of light and instinctively crouched down and disappeared into the shrubbery at the edge of the path. The sun had set about an hour ago, and a light rain sprinkled down from the heavens. She had been tracking her next assignment, a thief. He had stolen from a village, and the King wanted him dead. She was an assassin, the most skilled in her kingdom. And this thief was supposedly the most slippery. He had stolen hundreds of times, and this time he made the mistake of stealing from the King.

She slowly inched forward, still on her knees. As she got

closer to the source of light, she realized it was a campfire. She saw the outline of a body sitting next to it. That was him, the target. She carefully moved closer and closer, staying in the shadows of the tree line along the clearing in which he had settled. She heard a stick crack from behind her and she froze. She slowly turned her head, only to be faced with a curious fox that was now watching her. She shifted her gaze from the fox back to the clearing. There was no time for distractions.

She moved closer to her target, ever so carefully. He was sitting with his back to her, but she could tell he matched the description: Tall, muscular, dark hair. That was all she had gotten as a lead, but that was all she needed. She stood up swiftly, placing her hand on her hilt. The figure in front of her stiffened. As she took a step forward, he lunged. He jumped up from his seat and swung at her with his golden blade, the one he had stolen from the King. She easily dodged his attack and countered by hitting him in the side with the flat of her sword. He stumbled back, using that against him, she knocked her shoulder against his chest and threw him against a tree. His sword flew out of his hand and she held her own to his throat.

She let out a deep breath. One last time. Then it was done. She carefully cleaned off her blade and started back the way she had come after disposing of the body. That would be the last time. Or, it was, until the King gave her the next assignment.

Springs in the Wasteland

By Emily Peterson (Finalist)

There is no water to be found anywhere but the ocean. It's all we fight for, it's all we live for-- hey, we're even composed of about 75% of it. But still, we can't find it. Still, we starve for it. My head is swimming on a dry beach, and I only have a few days left until lack of water causes my swimming to stop. I didn't think it would be that way.

Every time we find a well, it's either dried up or doesn't have enough to satisfy all of us. We are condemned to wander the earth hunting this elusive prey. A small caravan preached to us about living water, but so far we haven't found whatever well they have. They're all dead now, besides, so I'd like to see whatever living water they got into.

Our town's last well dried up about two months ago if my math is right. We were forced to cross what was once the fruited plain to find whatever we could. But even the dirt is dying.

My mom said that there is a white house, somewhere in this vast desolate place. That has green gardens and a well that has not run dry. She said in it are the people that can save us. A mysterious Leader will reach out his warm hand, and in it will be a cup of clean water. We have to cling to that hope.

Because our mouths are so parched, we gave up on talking a few weeks ago. Instead of burying our dead, we leave them covered in a blanket. We can't afford to sweat. Our city of 200,000 has dwindled down to 200. Each day is longer and deadlier.

It's night; we've wandered the wasteland, and we've found nothing. The stars light up everything. In the city, LED would drown them out. Now there is nothing that could drown anything.

The light of the stars illuminates a figure walking towards us. The wind kicks up dust, and for a few minutes, the figure is but a shadow. I feel like I'm dying, and maybe this is another ghost. But once the time passes and the dust subdues, the figure is no ghost. He is a man, with a canteen in each hand.

I cry out and regret it. The pain in my throat makes me heave and double over. I look to the others, who are already asleep or dead. The morning will reveal the survivors, as it always does. I lift my eyes to the man, and he gives me one of the canteens.

His brown eyes smile at me. It's strange to see eyes that aren't red and swollen.

"I have this for you."

I move as much as I can, my limbs aching. I cannot walk another step. Unless this man has enough water to replenish me, somehow I know I will soon join the 199,800 from our city.

He completes the distance between us and opens the canteen for me. My trembling, dry, swollen hands grasp the canteen, and I lift it to what is left of my lips.

But no water meets my mouth.

I look in the canteen, and there is only a slip of paper. In distress, I look at the man. He gestures to the canteen.

I tip it and try to read but I can't. The man gently takes it from my hands and moves next to me.

"This is the living water they spoke of," he begins. I want to shout again. Look what living water did to them, I wanted to say. The preachers and the saints died faster than the rest of us. All the living water did was put a smile on their face when we threw their blankets over them. We don't need that hope. We need life.

"It's okay," he tries to comfort me as if he can read my mind, "This will give you a hope and a future."

If I could I would roll my eyes.

"See, I am doing a new thing," he reads, "'Now it springs up; do you not perceive it? I am making a way in the wilderness and streams in the desert.' Those streams can be yours," he finishes and opens the other canteen. In it is water. Not much, but enough to make me grab it and painfully cry once more. The water is cool in my mouth, and I try to drink the entire thing. But then when I look in the canteen, there's more than when I first drank.

"There is a way out of this wilderness," he tells me, "Get up, let's follow it."

"Who are you," my voice croaks out.

"There's more on the paper," he explains, his brown eyes falling to the paper. I notice how worn it is. He must have read it many times. Maybe to other people like me. "'For God so loved the world that He gave His only begotten Son, that whoever believes in Him shall not perish but have eternal life.'. Another, "Everyone who drinks this water will be thirsty again,"

I cough, trying to laugh.

"Let me continue. 'But whoever drinks the water I give them will never thirst. Indeed, the water I give them will become in them a spring of water welling up to eternal life."

My eyes burn, and I reach up and wipe away grainy tears that are bathed in next to nothing. He takes my hand and wipes away my tears with a clean cloth. I don't know where he got it, but it's wonderful to feel something soft and clean again.

"They did die, but they lived again," he exclaims and laughs once more. His laugh was the first I've heard in a year. I try to smile, but it hurts too much.

"He sees your pain," he tells me, and lifts the canteen to my lips once more, "He wants to give you springs in the wasteland."

The Doorbell

By Daniela Cantu (Finalist)

I sat against the bottom of our grey, moth-bitten sofa. The fire flickered dimly in its place, its warmth bathing the front of my face, chest, and legs. The clean, fluffy mess at the top of my head was being combed through by Ashley's thin, knobby fingers, her nails catching the rebel knots of dirty blond hair that had strayed her path along the way.

I tilted my shaggy head up from her palm half-heartedly and glanced towards the indent she had made on the couch. Her raven-stranded hair was pulled back behind her ears, frizzy strands of wispy hair sitting curly on her forehead.

Her eyes weren't focused on mine. Instead, they concentrated on the book in her hand, flipped pages mimicking the sound of the fire. Discontent with not keeping her focus, I rested my jaw on her knee, rolling my chin over the cap.

Her eyes flickered towards mine and narrowed in a smug glee, and she moved her thumb to brush it over my cheekbone.

""What's wrong?"" She asked softly, half of a laugh thriving in her voice.

I could only return a smile. Reciprocating, she gave my hair another ferocious shake.

A doorbell rang in the distance, and Ashley's eyes shifted to follow. I turned my head towards the noise and let out a slight muttery noise of stroke turmoil. Ashley rested her hand on my head for a delicate moment before standing up and walking towards the front door of the spacious apartment. I quickly stood from my position and tailed her, occasionally brushing against her side.

She opened the door, and I waited behind her, keeping my head leaning towards the door.

I eyed her thumb brushing against the peephole's slot and attempted to slot my hand against hers, something that she quickly brushed away. As unsurprising as the motion was, it frustrated me enough to press further against her, which still didn't seem like enough to shake her from squinting into the outlook of our apartment.

I frowned, a soft noise of confusion sprouting from my lower throat. There stood a man who looked to be about eight feet tall. His posture was lanky and unnatural underneath his bulky black trenchcoat. His skin was wrinkled and leathery, a dark, whole black. I could see throbbing veins from underneath his thin skin like they were screaming to be removed. My eyes panned up to his face. His head was completely bald but as leathery and veiny as the rest of his coated body. His lips were spread from ear-to-ear in a twisted smile, the indentions in his mouth chapped and split, his charred lips beaten and burnt to a crisp. Its eyes were wide and white, almost as if a thick filmy fog had been cast over it, showering its glare over white pupils. It also had no nose. Instead, a slight dip rested where it should be as if it had been carved out. Just looking at the thing made a spine-tingling chill run down my spine.

I tilted my head up to Ashley's, wanting to know how she reacted to this thing, searching for a crevice I could fill to protect her. I was used to seeing reactions created by a similar cause. Her responses would be taut and nimble, tiny yelps in surprise and anguish falling from her mouth without delay or hesitation. She would squeeze me close as I struggled to break free from her tenacious grip. I guess a way to describe that look and stressed movements would be fear, and based on the face of the thing, that should be her reaction, right?

Incorrect. Ashley passed me a confused and uninterpretable expression, and it looked as if it were passing through the beast. 'Can she not see it?' I pondered internally, and I watched Ashley tilt her head towards me from the thing. She chuckled lowly, shaking her head; strands of stray, rebel black hair fell onto her shoulders from the motion of the loose bun.

""Shy, I think we've been ding-dong ditched."" She hummed, leaning downwards to make eye contact with me. ""Maybe you could search for the kids and track them down."" She joked.

I stared at her, dumbfounded. ""Can you not see it?"" I whispered, staring over towards Ashley. She looked down at me, confused, before laughing.

""There's nothing there, Shy. Let's go back."" Ashley stated, gently tugging on my shoulder. I stood still, unmoving, completely dumbfounded. ""Can you not see it? Look."" I exclaimed, frustrated.

Our next-door neighbor gently pushed their door open, tiredly stepping out to glance over. Christ, I didn't think that I had been that loud. Ashley dragged me back into the house, swearing underneath frustrated huffs of air. ""What's gotten into you?""

Before she could close the door, I looked back towards the thing, falling silent. I swear I saw the thing's cracked, ashy, split lips split into a bloodcurdling, horrific grin. My stomach twisted into knots.

We were back in the same position we were a few minutes ago, her hand threading rows in my shaggy hair. My eyes weren't transfixed on her; they were on the wall next to the crackling fire; the spots of flicking flame engulfed into nothing along the border. The thing had consumed the fire flickering, its presence overwhelming that of the fires.

I stared at it, my heart thumping frantically in my chest, mimicking that of a frantic hummingbird's wings. It stared back, its eyes wide and unmoving, unnerving above its twisted, horrific grin. It sat there, just staring. The only thing that seemed to be moving was its pulsing veins, sickening to watch. I noticed Ashley's hand shift in my hair, doubling back towards her leg in a resting manner, and I flinched, snapping my shagged head towards her.

She looked down, her eyebrows jumping a hurdle of surprise. Then, she tilted her head towards where I was staring, creases of confusion forming between her hurdled brows.

""Do you see it? Please, tell me, give me some sort of a sign that you can!"" I frantically spoke, my voice shaking in my raw throat. She gave me another confused look. I knew she was surprised at my frantic babbling because she shot me a look of concern.

""What's there? What do you see?"" She asked softly, reaching her hand down to reassure me. I snapped my gaze towards her, and she flinched her hand back, eyes widening in disbelief.

""Stop trying to reassure me! I'm not crazy!"" I barked at her, frustration filling my body.

I scampered from her, racing towards the throbbing figure, growling out threats that were weak in my mind from fear.

""Leave us alone, I can see you!"" I screamed, throwing myself at the being, which disappeared, and I ultimately passed through it, smashing a vase that rested on the fireplace's outer rim.

""Oh my god, Shiloh."" Ashley groaned loudly, her stare flickering towards my quivering body. I looked down at my hand; it was bleeding.

She grabbed me by the scruff of my neck and started to tug me away as I continued to howl furiously, fighting and clawing at the thing, furious. Why wouldn't she let me protect her? It was dangerous. It was coming closer!

""I have no idea what's gotten into you, Shiloh."" She huffed. I couldn't keep my eyes off of it. It was approaching, its twisted limbs contorting as it crept. My disgust towards it only seemed to increase with every bit of movement made and abnormal bodily function. Despite this, I couldn't help but stare into it further. Its veins throbbed rapidly and exceptionally, bones threatening to tear through leathery skin. Its lips spread into a wicked grin, hundreds of bloodstained, needle-thin teeth showing through its split lips. A thick velocity of horror escaped me.

I was dragged off into my room, a shin gently shoving me further inside. The door shut before I could turn back around. I clawed at the door, my nails digging into the wooden mold. I was screaming, my hoarse yells quieting as my throat cracked and burned. Ashley's footsteps began to grow faint.

Then, everything went quiet.

Then, it wasn't.

I heard a loud, thick scream that cut through the suffocating silence, and I started weeping, clawing at the door. The screams never seemed to end but crescendo. Finally, I collapsed on the ground, screaming in chorus with Ashley. My shaken vision twitched down towards my tiny, clawed, hairy legs, screaming even louder until the only thing that filled the air was my own hollering.

As I stared at my small, furry limbs, my barking growing faint into whimpers, I began to wish that I had hands.

The Girl With Moths in her Hair

By Chloe Thompson (Finalist)

I always hated summer break. The endless days that seem to last the length of a slow week, the loneliness of the farm that I have come to call home, and the eerie silence of the Montanan countryside. When I was ten my parents died in a drunk driving incident and I had been sent to live with my closest living relative, on a farm with my great uncle. The farm house is squeezed between a dense forest and acres upon acres of tall wheat plants. The nearest store is 19 miles away and my uncle is just about the only other person I see during summer breaks. Every day I drown in the boredom that engulfs me like the logs in a campfire. I read, chase barn cats, and draw pictures of my old life in sad detail. My uncle is a very quiet and reserved man, his only rule for me is that I don't venture too deeply into the forest or the wheat field.

Sometime in late June my uncle was out in the fields working and I was pretending to be a pirate, the big red barn next to the hill that leads to the forest my pirate ship, when I saw a swarm of moths circling something on the forest floor. I hate moths but my curiosity got the best of me and I ran up the hill only to see a girl sitting on the muddy ground, giggling at the moths that surrounded her. I walked up behind her slowly, which caused the moths to fly away in a fright and the young girl to turn around. I could feel my hands sweating as we first made eye contact.

"Oh, hello, I was just speaking to my friends, sorry if they spooked you" she said cheerfully.

"Ta-talking to them?" I questioned.

The girl giggled "Why yes! They tell me the things they see from the sky and they listen to me as I talk. I believe they are the only creatures who truly listen to me".

The girl was about my age. She wore a beautiful white dress and had brown butterfly clips in her hair that more closely resembled moths than butterflies. "So, what's your name?" She asked.

"Uh, I'm Ben. My parents were hoping for a son but when I came out a girl they just decided to keep the name. What's your name?"

Her smile faded "I have been here so long I can't remember my name, I don't even remember the sound of my mothers voice. Hey!" her smile returned "maybe you can help me pick out a name!"

"Alright! How about..." I thought back to the book I was reading for inspiration "Quinn!"

"I love it! What do you say? Do you want to be friends? We

can play together and I can introduce you to the moths!"

"Ok! You can eat dinner with my uncle and I, and we can have sleepovers in my room!"

"No!" she looked scared now. "You can never NEVER tell your uncle about me ok? Pinky promise?" I was confused but I didn't want to lose my only friend by pushing for further answers so I pinky promised her. From then on, I spent my days in the base of the forest playing with Quinn and her moths. We would play pretend, read, draw together, and simply talk, but I was never allowed to ask her about where she lived or who she was. And that was ok.

One day before I went inside to eat dinner with my uncle, Quinn looked at me seriously and said "Ben, I really need to show you something. Tomorrow night I need you to sneak outside and meet me at the edge of the wheat field. Bring a flashlight and DO NOT let your uncle find out. See you tomorrow night." Before I could protest she was gone, running back into the forest. At first I wasn't going to do it, but she was my new best friend and it seemed she needed help.

So the next night I quietly snuck out of the house with my biggest flashlight. When Quinn saw me approaching she jumped up and down with excitement, giggling like a happy baby. Quinn grabbed my hand. "Are you ready?" She smiled.

"I guess" I responded. Quinn grabbed my hand and started sprinting into the wheat field. "No!" I yelled, still running "I am not allowed to be in here! My uncle will be so mad!"

"Just trust me!" Screamed Quinn, and we ran, and ran, and ran until she came to a sudden stop. "We're here," she said. In front of us was a small, run-down shack that I hadn't known existed. "You go in first," whispered Quinn. Curiously I stepped forward and opened the door. My flashlight shone on the splintery wooden walls. The only things in the room were a tool bench, a strange deep pit in the middle of the room, and of course, hundreds of moths.

I turned around to say something to Quinn but she was gone, in her place stood my uncle with a blank face looking down at me. "I told you not to come here" he groaned "why can't you just listen".

"What is this place?" I questioned.

"I didn't want to have to do this to you Ben" He said, and In one swift motion he picked me up and looked at me "I am so sorry" He quickly dropped me into the pit. I screamed as I heard him walk away, begging him to help me but as I gathered my bearings in that hole I realized what was in there with me. Dead, dusty moths lined the floor, scraps of white fabric that crumbled to the touch, and one thin piece of paper with Quinn's picture on it. It was a newspaper titled "MISSING: Laila Flannagen last seen May 30th 1992".

It only took me three days of sitting in that pit alone to understand what Quinn, or should I say Laila, had meant about the moths being the only creatures to truly listen and to share secrets about what they see from the sky. Or maybe, I was just going crazy.

The Happiest Days of Our Lives

By Andrew Davies (Finalist)

The food bowl sits empty in the kitchen as the man lies
motionless in his chair.

It's been this way for two days already, and for two days,
the man has lain there in the living room, slumped over, head
strangely turned up to the ceiling, and silent. His television set
across from him is still playing those flashy colors and bodiless
voices. Blaring through the night, ceaseless. For two days, I
haven't eaten.

Now as I lie before the old man with my long nose nestled
between forepaws, watching patiently, it occurs to me that
something isn't quite right here. The man hasn't moved a bit
since I found him this way. He is sitting completely still. His skin
is so loose. Loose as though his muscles underneath have
shriveled and expired, and all there is to define him is the frame
of his skeleton. I notice that his complexion has gone paler,
softer, too. I notice his veins outlining through his knuckles,
running up the insides of his arms. I see the man's hair. It's long,
drained white, but sparse, and spotted with blemishes. Then I

see the man's face. His eyes. Dried. The color that once swam through them is no longer there. And he's staring at something in the air, I can't see it, but the man seems so captivated since he's been sitting there and looking at it for days. Or, perhaps, he's staring at nothing.

I don't know. I don't know much of anything, really. I know that the man is old, and he moves in gradual, unsteady motions, and struggles as he walks. And when he is tired, he is exhausted, and he stops and rests and heaves for air like he's on the verge of collapsing. And sometimes, the man returns to his bed and sleeps for a while. The man's ways confuse me, but so long as I get my food and drink—and my head pats—I'm happy.

The man hasn't been himself, though. He should have moved, at least twitched a little, by now.

I stand up and I yelp at him.

He doesn't move.

I yelp louder.

Nothing.

I bark at the man. I bark again. I haven't spoken like this to him in years.

I'm met only with shaming silence, so I slink away from him apologetically. I recompose myself. Then I look up to him again. And I set my chin carefully on his knee. I just want him to acknowledge me. But it seems I've disappointed him somehow. He remains aimlessly staring off into space, and his tongue is hanging slightly out from his mouth now, mocking me.

I draw nearer to the man, I investigate him more closely. I outstretch my neck and run my nose through his clothing, sniffing viciously. I can smell the stink emanating from him, a putrid rotting smell. Then I repugnantly pull my nose away and only look him over again. His chest isn't moving.

Then I realize—this is a game. The man is testing me. He's testing my loyalty to him, the integrity of my companionship. This is a test of patience and commitment, and until I prove to him my goodness, he won't move a hair for me. Of course. How could I be so stupid? I can't just lie around like a buffoon and expect the man to reward me for nothing. I have to earn my keep. And I can tell by the dumb expression showing on his face that I'm not impressing him so far. Damn it. I'm better than this. I have to think of something.

Think, think, think.

Then I've got it.

I step up to the man, ears perked, excitement shivering out my tail. I lift my forelegs, then shakily rise on my hind legs and, for a moment, I am balanced standing tall like the man does. Then I drop back to all fours. I wait for the man's reaction. Still a blank stare. Dry apathy. Still unimpressed.

My stomach groans. I need to work harder.

I drop to the floor and roll over back and forth. I rise, then spin in a circle. I army crawl across the floor. I snatch a rubber dogbone from beside the man's chair and I bite down on it to make that squeaking noise that it always makes. Next I reach out a paw and gesture for him to take it so we can engage in a handshake like the man does with other men, but when I touch his hand, it slips away from me.

He doesn't even say anything. Like I don't exist.

Another day passes. I'm growing weaker. My head feels clouded with perpetual delirium. I don't know what else I could do to prove my loyalty. I know I am loyal to him. I've never disobeyed his command, never been insubordinate. And still he sits there, unmoving, giving me no attention at all.

Maybe I deserve this. I just can't figure out why.

Now his face is going yellow. A thick, rank stench pervades the air around him. There is a fly buzzing about his head, it momentarily lands on his eye and settles there.

The decrepit meat hanging off his bones looks so inviting. But I need to restrain myself—that is what good boys do, anyway. And as I sit before him, I remember a time when the man didn't look so unalive.

Once there was a time when the man would release me into the backyard and he would hurl a tennis ball into the green. He would urge me to fetch it, and he'd smile, and his hair was darker and full. Then when I'd retrieve the ball and return it, the thing lathered with saliva, he would take it and toss it out again. Dexterous and sweeping, merely an old man in his becoming. A relic that did not yet hold value.

I didn't much see the value in anything back then, how temporary it all was.

The Mournful Tragedy of Walter Dormio

By John Colby Andrews (Finalist)

Yorkshire is such a puzzling town. Bright, lively, and vibrating by day, yet quiet, cold and empty by night. How can the positions of a star change such a place? How can it be the cause for blends of polar opposites? Blends, blends are evident; quiet, dark, cold, yet one man who could be considered a mouse scurrying for its final scrap of food before its hiding scrapes his shoes down the streets. Walter Dormio is your average 30-year-old British character; careless, hunched, and smoking a cig. No family to knock on the door to, no wife to share a bed with, no money to spend on leisures of alcohol or prostitutes, just a sad man with no possibility of blocking out the screeching dreadful sounds of life ringing in his ears.

For the past two nights, Walter has experienced episodes of unfortunate but bizarrely repetitive images in his sleep. What could almost be summed as horrific premonitions that are attempted to be ignored by him, they continue to be crammed in the back of his head, popping up here and there every few minutes, like that fly at a lampstand. No one would want to accept these dreams as premonitions, but Walter has a small suspicion that these are no longer dreams and lights flashing from God's headlight, signaling LOOK OUT in morse code. These dreams, in question, include images of death, deterioration, and blood, with the time "21/6/98 2:36 AM". June 21, 1998, 2:36 in the black morning, only 5 hours and 21 minutes away from now.

Though he desperately tries every minute to repress these dreams, they begin to lurk every corner of every street he walks down. Everywhere he goes, he is reminded of that exact time. Even if one would rub their eyes and put on their specs, it would seem that time would stay on that street sign, it would be muttered in a busy bakery, it would be a motif in a schizophrenic episode. Dormio is losing his mind, he fears some external or natural force would kill him at this exact time; something so bad would happen, something so inevitable and unavoidable would grab his veins at this precise moment. Should he sleep through the night? It was an option, but the thought stirring through his head is too warm to be frozen on a pillow. Dormio can't ask for help, people would call him crazy. Even so, who would listen to him? Is this just a case of someone so frustrated by the festering dread of isolation? No one knows except himself.

The time is 1:45 AM, the same day as the premonition. Dormio presses the back of his head against the wall in his bedroom. He sits next to his bed on the floor, profusely sweating. In a room so quiet, where you'd imagine a pin drop would wake a heavy sleeper, inside the head of Walter, noises that are louder than a circus fire circles his head like a children's amusement ride. The voices, the voices, the voices are too much for him. The voices, the voices, the voices are only repeating over and over that dreadful timestamp. There is no possible way out of hell, Walter feels so helpless stacked on top of what feels like dead bodies muttering their final words. Such a horrifying image that can only be kept inside the head of Walter, because once again, his bed is empty, he has no one to kiss when he comes home, he has no one to engage with. The only engagement he gets is from the noises torturing him, and he wants them to leave.

As Walter starts to lose the track of time, and aimlessly falls down his own consciousness as the voices don't stop to breathe, he twirls his head in a plea to shake them out. As what feels like ages pass by, Walter fears something never considered before: no end. How someone can so quickly go from the fear of an end to a fear of no end is a question for scholars, but it made complete sense to Dormio. He grabs the gun he keeps under his bed, and, staring down the barrel like a stalker fixating through the keyhole of whom he's admiring, starts to sweat even more. The voices are louder and louder, and there is no light he can use to burn away the webs he's tangled in. In a final glimpse of hope, he pulls the trigger and paints the wall in his own, passionate, dark red blood staining every nook of that plane. Though the voices are considerably louder, it seems the gunshot is what woke the neighbors. Crowded inside the room, watching a lifeless, helpless body contorted and slump against the wall, detectives could easily rule it as a suicide, while never suspecting the sounds plaguing that very man they look down at.

Walter James Dormio, age 30, death by suicide on June 21, 1998, 2:36 AM

Cool Imagination Titles

Convergence by Brian Claspell
Jim Conrad may not be as fictional as the CIA thinks. Pick up *Convergence*, a mystery-thriller, on Amazon and at other fine retailers.

One Spark - *Short Story Anthology 2011-2018*
Enjoy reading the short stories of all the winners (2011-2018) and 2018 finalist of the "Imagination Begins with You…" high school writing contest. All proceeds support scholarships.

One Spark – *"Imagination Begins with You…" 2019*
Jump into reading finalist stories from the "Imagination Begins with You…" high school writing contest. All proceeds support scholarships.

One Spark – *"Imagination Begins with You…" 2020*
"Imagination Begins with You…" high school writing contest is an annual writing contest open. The finalist and winners are published in an annual short story collection where all proceeds support scholarships. Enjoy!

One Spark – *"Imagination Begins with You…" 2021*
Full of amazing stories from young writers in the "Imagination Begins with You…" high school writing contest. 100% of proceeds support writing scholarships.

One Spark- *"Imagination Begins with You…" 2022*
A collection of stories from young writers in the "Imagination Begins with You…" high school writing contest. All proceeds support writing scholarships.

Made in the USA
Columbia, SC
26 August 2022

65453630R00111